MW00831497

04

Thea in Dreamland

SPY CLASSROOM

code name
DREAMSPEAKER

SPY CLASSROOM

code name
PANDEMONIUM

code name
GLINT

A Girl Being Seductive ♥

code name
FLOWER GARDEN

SPY

CLASSROOM

04

Thea in Dreamland

Takemachi

ILLUSTRATION BY **Tomari**

YEN ON

New York

SPY CLASSROOM 04

Translation by Nathaniel Thrasher
Cover art by Tomari
Assistance with firearm research: Asaura

This book is a work of fiction. Names, characters, places, and incidents are the product of the author's imagination or are used fictitiously. Any resemblance to actual events, locales, or persons, living or dead, is coincidental.

SPY KYOSHITSU Vol. 4 <<YUMEGATARI>> NO TEIA
©Takemachi, Tomari 2020
First published in Japan in 2020 by KADOKAWA CORPORATION, Tokyo.
English translation rights arranged with KADOKAWA CORPORATION, Tokyo through TUTTLE-MORI AGENCY, INC., Tokyo.

English translation © 2022 by Yen Press, LLC

Yen On
150 West 30th Street, 19th Floor
New York, NY 10001

Visit us at yenpress.com
facebook.com/yenpress
twitter.com/yenpress
yenpress.tumblr.com
instagram.com/yenpress

First Yen On Edition: September 2022
Edited by Yen On Editorial: Anna Powers
Designed by Yen Press Design: Andy Swist, Wendy Chan

Yen On is an imprint of Yen Press, LLC.
The Yen On name and logo are trademarks of Yen Press, LLC.

The publisher is not responsible for websites (or their content) that are not owned by the publisher.

Library of Congress Cataloging-in-Publication Data
Names: Takemachi, author. | Tomari, Meron, illustrator. | Thrasher, Nathaniel Hiroshi, translator.
Title: Spy classroom / Takemachi ; illustrated by Tomari ; translation by Nathaniel Thrasher.
Other titles: Spy kyoushitsu. English
Description: First Yen On edition. | New York, NY : Yen On, 2021.
Identifiers: LCCN 2021021119 | ISBN 9781975322403 (v. 1 ; trade paperback) |
    ISBN 9781975322427 (v. 2 ; trade paperback) | ISBN 9781975338824
    (v. 3 ; trade paperback) | ISBN 9781975338848 (v. 4 ; trade paperback)
Subjects: | CYAC: Spies—Fiction. | Schools—Fiction.
Classification: LCC PZ7.1.T343 Sp 2021 | DDC [Fic]—dc23
LC record available at https://lccn.loc.gov/2021021119

ISBNs: 978-1-9753-3884-8 (paperback)
       978-1-9753-3885-5 (ebook)

1 2022

LSC-C

Printed in the United States of America

CONTENTS

Prologue

Purple Ant ①

"My dear Spider, what would you say is the most human thing a person can do?"

The United States of Mouzaia was the largest superpower in the world.

Instead of participating in the Great War directly, its role had been confined to selling weapons and supplies to its allied nations. As the war dragged on, their economy gained a major boost, and with how much of the world was still recovering from their war scars nowadays, they had become the center of the global economy.

It was no exaggeration to say that the world revolved around the United States.

Over on its west coast, it had a city named Mitario filled with skyscrapers and people strolling its streets enjoying its prosperity. Cheering could be heard from the sports bars when the baseball relay broadcasts were on TV, and young people would frequently ride the subway to head to music halls and advance screenings of black-and-white films at luxury high-rises more than fifty stories tall.

A pair of peculiar men stood in Mitario.

They were up on the observation deck of the Westport Building, a skyscraper that sat right in the heart of the city. The observation deck was a tourist attraction on its forty-seventh floor, but it was closed for the day, so the two of them were the only ones there.

One of them, a man with a mushroom-shaped hairdo, let out an impressed sigh as he stared at the skyline full of high-rises. Even in his expensive suit, his easygoing expression and aggressively fungal hairstyle prevented him from giving any impression of dignity.

He was White Spider, a spy from the Galgad Empire.

The man beside him wore a cheery look on his face as he asked his question. After a few moments of silence, he offered his own answer. "It's when they leave behind their dying words, you see. Humans are the only creatures who can picture what the world will look like after their death, and they're the only ones who can leave their thoughts behind in the form of speech."

"Man, those buildings are really something."

"...Spider, are you even listening to me?"

"Sorry, it's my first time here. I gotta say, Purple Ant, I'm pretty jealous that you get to work in such a nice—"

White Spider felt something graze his cheek.

A staticky noise buzzed out, and by the time White Spider reacted, his beloved hair was already singed.

He collapsed onto the floor with a yelp. "What the hell?! You nearly zapped me to death there!"

"Your reactions are just as spineless as ever, I see," the man called Purple Ant replied, still holding his stun gun. "It's your own fault for not paying attention. You deserve to die thrice over for that."

The man had a distinct gentleness about him, and his face was so kindly, he looked suited for a job in a preschool or as a nurse. Unlike White Spider, he looked right at home in his double-breasted, navy-blue suit and his stylish hat. His eyes were constantly smiling beneath his long forelocks.

He was Purple Ant, another Galgad spy.

Just like White Spider, he was a member of the spy team Serpent making covert moves across the world.

"Your stories are always so long, though," White Spider said unrepentantly. He stood back up and dusted off his clothes. "Anyway, I'm here about work."

"Work? Oh, how boorish."

"What's so boorish about coming to a spy and talking shop?"

"Well, here I was, thinking you'd come to see me out of sheer love for an older teammate."

"Yeah, no."

White Spider scratched his head and looked down through the window at the lower floors.

"The Tolfa Economic Conference is going to start next month in the Westport Building and go on for half a year. They gave it a big, fancy name, but what it comes down to is a bunch of companies and bureaucrats from the Allies are getting together and duking it out over their rights. The whole continent of Tolfa's been a mess ever since the war, and the Allies want to figure out how they're going to divvy up the pie."

"Nauseating, isn't it?" Purple Ant muttered.

Tolfa was a continent that the developed countries had been controlling through colonial rule. Galgad had once had colonies there itself, but after losing the war, it had been forced to relinquish them to the Allies. A decade had passed since the war's end, but the Allies were still squabbling among themselves over who had the rights to which parts of Tolfa.

Now they were holding an extended conference to discuss those very rights—and not a single Tolfan nation had been invited to the table.

Purple Ant sighed. "So you want me to manipulate the conference to serve the Empire's ends?"

"No, I'm gonna handle that myself. I have a different job for you." White Spider gave him a look. "Spies from all over the world are going to be there. The Fend Commonwealth's CIM will dispatch their entire Retias team, and the Bumal Kingdom is sure to send Shadowseed and the Goosefoot Sisters. Mouzaia's intelligence agency, the JJJ, will have their cream of the crop there as well, so you'll need to take special care with the Giraffe and the Turtle. And we still don't know who this 'Ouka' spy is, but with how big the conference is going to be, there's no way they don't drop by. We're talking a full roster of international all-stars."

White Spider grinned.

"I want them all dead."

Purple Ant rubbed the back of his neck. "That's a little grisly, don't you think?"

Theirs was an era of spies operating behind the scenes. With a conference that long and with that much on the line, it was impossible to say just how many spies would end up attending it. If you counted the ones from Mouzaia's intelligence agency, the number would probably break four digits.

Purple Ant's instructions were as simple as they were cruel—get rid of everyone who stood in their way as quickly as possible.

"Massacring people is such inelegant work," Purple Ant went on. "I thought our trade was supposed to be about *controlling* people, not killing them."

"Maybe, but taking people alive is hardly your specialty."

"………"

"I can count on you, right? Word is, you might have to deal with that rising star from Din's Foreign Intelligence Office, too—Bonfire."

"Ah." Purple Ant nodded.

The Din Republic had been dealing bitter defeats to the Galgad Empire for years, and by the sound of it, the Republic would be joining the fray as well. Despite their status as a minor rural nation, the influence they held over world affairs made their attendance all but inevitable. And as rumor had it, the man in question—Bonfire—was a monster the likes of which were rarely seen.

Purple Ant beamed and lashed out with his stun gun.

White Spider dodged at the last moment and let out a pathetic shriek. "Again with this shit! You gotta stop trying to zap me for no reason, man!"

"Your tone was pompous. You deserve to die thrice over for that."

"...I'm pretty sure I was just talking normally."

"By my standards, it was pompous." Purple Ant took the stun gun he was holding directly in front of White Spider's face and squeezed it until it broke. "Don't you worry about me. Here in Mitario, I'm the king."

White Spider's expression was still frozen, and Purple Ant gave him a big smile.

"Hard to believe it's already been a month since we had that conversation. Oh, how time flies."

Purple Ant let out a long exhale as he sat in his base of operations, a members-only underground bar. It was a quiet little room with dim, indirect lighting and a modest bar counter. Only a few people in all of Mitario knew about it.

He took a sip of his cola. He didn't care much for alcohol.

He had spent the past month carrying out countless assassinations. Between spies and secret policemen, he was already responsible for forty-eight kills, and not a single person had any idea about his special talent. Nobody would ever be able to find him.

Plus, he'd accomplished something else that day, as well.

"Can I get you anything, miss? A beer, maybe?"

He turned to the individual he'd forced to sit in the seat beside him. She writhed in pain.

"Oh, that's right." Purple Ant offered her a bow. "You have that hole in your chest. I'm so sorry for making such a thoughtless offer to a lady such as yourself. I like to consider myself a gentleman, you know."

The expression of his "companion" was one of agony. Sweat streamed down her face, and if looks could kill, the hateful glare she gave him from beneath her disheveled hair would have done just that. Blood trickled from the hole in her side as she pressed down on it.

"You're a spy from the Din Republic, aren't you? I must say, you're a lot younger than I expected you to be. Can I ask your name?"

"..............."

"Hrmm, that's quite a problem. I would think you could at least *introduce* yourself."

He groaned. He considered listening to people's dying words to be his life's work, but he so rarely managed to capture people alive. It would've been a damn shame to kill her without listening to what she had to say.

"Are you waiting for someone to come save you, perhaps?"

"..............."

"It's Bonfire you're waiting for, isn't it? Ah, but I suppose you and your friends call him 'Klaus.' Oh, no, it's quite all right. I was actually hoping he'd come here as well."

"..............."

"Let's have a little chat while we wait for him. We can reminisce on this whole thing from start to finish—from when you and your friends first took me on to the moment of your ignoble defeat."

Purple Ant gave his captive a smile.

"And then, when we're done…we'll see if I can guess your name."

There wasn't so much as a sliver of hope to be found in that process. Only despair.

"Now then," Purple Ant said, "let's start with how you all got to Mouzaia."

Chapter 1

Mobilizing

The world was awash in pain.

Ten years had passed since the end of the Great War, the largest war in human history. Seeing its horrors had driven the world's politicians to turn to spy work rather than military might as their preferred way of influencing other countries.

Nations the world over poured resources into their intelligence agencies, leading to an age of shadow wars fought between spies.

Lamplight was a spy team that fought on behalf of the Din Republic.

Their current goal was to root out a mysterious intelligence organization called Serpent. During one of their domestic missions, they had succeeded in capturing a spy with information on the group, and upon learning that Serpent was going to make a move in the United States of Mouzaia, they decided to head there as part of their search.

First, though, they had to make their preparations for the decisive battle that was to come.

Their previous missions had taken place at home and in the neighboring Galgad Empire, but this time around, the situation was totally different. Their destination, the United States, had a completely different language and culture than they did. Between making counterfeit passports, fabricating their career histories, and figuring out how they were going to procure firearms on-site, there were a million things they needed to do.

Normally, their anxiety about an upcoming mission would make the process a rather melancholy one.

This time, though, the whole team was in strangely high spirits.

As Thea walked down the hallway, she heard a scream from out in the garden.

"SHREEEEEEEEEEEEEEP!"

"...Huh?"

It sounded like someone was dying. That was the kind of blood-curdling scream people made only as their lives came to an end.

That said, what was a *"shreep"*?

Wh-what's going on over there?

She was in Heat Haze Palace, the gorgeous manor that served as Lamplight's main stronghold, and whatever had just happened, it had happened bright and early in the morning.

Thea tilted her head at the odd turn of events.

Her most distinctive features were her lustrous black hair and her curvy proportions. She was just eighteen years old, but you certainly wouldn't know it from her beauty and grace. Her code name was Dreamspeaker.

When she headed to the courtyard the scream had come from, she found a pair of girls glaring at each other.

"Ha! Today's 10K is mine," the white-haired one said.

"...Tch. You're such a muscle brain," her cerulean-haired opponent replied. "I'll have you know I could do another ten kilometers easy."

Ah, so the two of them had been racing.

"Heh. You wanna go? We can do our own triathlon—another 10K, then marksmanship, then sparring. Today's the day I take that title of Lamplight's Strongest off you."

A victorious grin spread across "Pandemonium" Sybilla's face as she panted heavily. Her distinctive features were her muscles, which were as toned as a wild animal's, and the dignified sharpness in her gaze.

"You think beating me in one lousy 10K means you're better than me? Bring it on."

The cool retort came from "Glint" Monika. With the exception of her asymmetrical cerulean hairdo, she had pruned every notable characteristic out of her medium build.

Sybilla and Monika continued bantering back and forth across the courtyard.

"Hey," Sybilla said, "lookin' at our 10K record, I'm in the lead."

"So what?" Monika shot back. "I had a couple bad days, that's all."

"Ha. That's a pretty lame excuse, comin' from you."

"Yeah, yeah, keep talking. Next time, you'll be eating my dust."

It sounded like they were arguing, but their eyes were filled with a competitive drive.

Tense as their battles were, they were all in good fun.

It begged the question, then, where had the scream come from?

"Up and at 'em, Lily. Time for another ten."

"Yeah, on your feet. No slacking."

"SHREEEEEEEP!"

Ah. As it turned out, the scream's source was collapsed in a heap on the ground. She leaped to her feet and rushed over to Thea all drenched in sweat.

"Thea, you gotta save me! They're trying to kill me!"

It was "Flower Garden" Lily, a silver-haired girl with a distinctively charming appearance and a voluptuous bosom. Technically speaking, she was the girls' leader.

Tears rolled down her face as she clung to Thea's hips.

"I'm gonna die! I really am! They keep making me run 10Ks first thing in the morning!"

"Hey!" Thea yelped. "Don't go sweating all over me!"

"This sweat is my soul, melted away. These demons are wringing out all my soul juice."

As Lily began talking nonsense, her teammates grabbed her by the shoulders.

"'Pologies for the inconvenience."

"We'll be on our way now."

After making some very professional-sounding comments, Sybilla and Monika dragged Lily off.

"Lily, you gotta keep up your training," Sybilla reminded her. "In our line of work, we need all the stamina we can get."

"I don't wanna! I wanna be the kind of spy who uses her *brain* to—"

"We've got another squad for that," Monika replied. "Our job is to deliver the brawn."

As Thea watched the other two cart Lily away like a suitcase, she recalled what the three of them had in common.

Together, they were the Operations squad—the subdivision of Lamplight that helped get the job done from the front lines.

By the look of it, morale among them was high.

Thea went back inside, and this time, it was the dining hall she heard voices from. Unlike the scream from earlier, the voices sounded harmonious and cheerful.

She decided to go have a look from the sidelines.

In the center, there was a girl with brown hair holding a book in one hand. "All right, question one hundred."

This was Sara, code name "Meadow." She was an adorable girl with unruly hair and big, round eyes like you might find on a woodland creature. She normally looked as timid as could be, but at the moment, her expression was sunny.

She cleared her throat, then raised her voice. "This is the last one, and it's pretty tricky, okay? The forty-seven-story Westport Building sits to the southwest of Mitario Station, and there's a rooftop garden on its eighth floor. If the target is sitting on the bench in the northernmost part of that garden, how many places are there to snipe them from? Please list them all within one minute."

The moment she finished, the two girls sitting across from her sprang into motion and quickly skimmed through the array of documents laid out on the table, flipping through multiple heavy books at the same time and jotting down pencil notes all the while.

The first girl to answer was the blond one.

"There's five! There's Lyment Hall and Nywengate Tower. The construction site right beside it would work, too. With a top-of-the-line sniper rifle, you could make the shot from Mitario Hotel. And if you snuck into the art hall's control room, you could snipe them from there!"

She was "Fool" Erna. Her skin was so pale, it almost seemed translucent, making her look like a doll.

After answering the question, she puffed up her chest with pride. Sara, the examiner, gave her a satisfied nod. "Great work! You got all of—"

"I found another one, yo."

Before Sara could finish her sentence, the ash-pink-haired girl cut her off. It was "Forgetter" Annette. Between her messily tied-up hair and her big eye patch, her appearance was rather striking.

"Starting next week, there'll be a circus staying at West Kopek Plaza. You could make the shot from on top of the tent."

"What?" Erna's eyes went wide with bewilderment. She hurriedly flipped back through the documents. "Th-there's no way. It's not tall enough to hit the garden from there."

"But the target's on the north bench, yo. It works out."

"What kind of sniper goes and climbs on top of a circus tent?!"

"I don't think we should let common sense hold us down."

"Wh-*what*?!"

Erna and Annette glared at each other, on the verge of coming to blows…

…but before that could happen, Sara clapped her hands. "It's okay— you're both right. That's full marks for both of you. Now what do you say we have some snacks as a reward for a job well done?"

Erna's and Annette's expressions immediately softened. "Oh?" "Don't mind if I do!" they replied, nodding as they headed peacefully to the kitchen.

That was when Sara finally noticed that Thea was there. She let out a small gasp of surprise. "Oh, Miss Thea. I didn't realize you were watching."

"I must say, that was incredible."

"Right? The two of them are so talented. Those questions were pretty tough, but they both got all of them right."

In a way, it made perfect sense.

The reasons Erna and Annette washed out of their academies had nothing to do with their technical abilities and everything to do with their catastrophically poor interpersonal skills. Now they were finally unlocking the potential they'd had inside them all along.

Sara slumped her shoulders in shame. "T-to be honest, they're both way better at all this than I am. It kind of bums me out…"

"Not at all. If anything, the way you're able to rein those two in is the most impressive skill of all."

"Hmm?"

As someone who'd been forced to go to great lengths to win those same two girls over, Thea had nothing but respect for what Sara had accomplished.

Sure enough, the three of them together really did feel like a cohesive unit.

Together, they were the Specialist squad—the group that used their highly versatile skills to provide the team with backup.

By the look of it, their spirits going into the mission were high as well.

Once she finished checking in on her teammates, the next place Thea went was the main hall.

Inside, there was a big map of their Mitario mission site hung up on one of the blackboards, and the map was littered with magnets holding up little notes.

A girl with red hair stood before it all. Her arms and legs were slender, and she had a sort of fragility about her that was reminiscent of a glass sculpture. Her name was Grete, and her code name was "Daughter Dearest."

"I checked in with the others," Thea said to her. "And they're doing swimmingly. If anything, I'm afraid all our prep work is going *too* well."

"That's wonderful to hear. Thank you for getting that done. There's nobody better than you at taking the group's emotional pulse, after all," Grete replied with a composed smile.

She and Thea were partners in crime.

Together, they were the Intel squad—the rearguard team that handled drawing up plans and giving orders to the others.

"The energy is fantastic. It's almost odd how excited everyone is," Thea said.

"Oh, I'm not surprised. It's the first time we've all been in one place in a long while."

Thea nodded.

That there was the reason behind their high morale—the fact that all eight of them were back together. After the bioweapon retrieval mission, the team had split up into two. Each group had been through harsh missions and constant tribulations, and the time they'd spent working separately had made them long for their missing teammates. There wasn't a single member of the team who didn't share that sentiment.

Furthermore, this mission was going to pit them against the sinister Serpent, the mysterious group that had slaughtered their Inferno predecessors. The Lamplight girls didn't know who exactly they would be up against, but they knew they were in for a fierce fight, and their nerves and enthusiasm were mixing together in the best possible way.

As a result, they were firing on all cylinders.

That's right...everyone's raring to go. Everyone, with one exception...

Thea felt a stabbing pain in her chest.

"...Thea?"

She heard Grete call her name.

She gasped. She hadn't heard a word Grete had been saying.

"Huh? What? I'm sorry, Grete. I zoned out there for a moment."

"...Is everything okay? You've been a little out of it these past few days. Maybe you ought to rest a little."

"N-no, I'm fine. It's nothing."

"Don't push yourself, all right? Remember, you'll be the one in charge of command and control this time around."

Hearing that sent another twinge through her chest.

Thea had been appointed as the team's commanding officer for the upcoming mission.

She and Grete would be sorting through the incoming intel together, but it was going to be her job to assign tasks to her teammates. The work she did would determine if their mission ended in success or failure.

But I—

She felt her blood run cold.

"Thea."

Then she heard someone behind her.

She turned around and was greeted by a tall, beautiful man with long hair. It was Klaus, Lamplight's boss.

"Would you mind heading out with me? There's something I want to show you."

◇◇◇

Thea did as Klaus said and followed him to the administrative district in the capital.

The area was right by the station, and the Cabinet Office and Ministry of Foreign Affairs buildings stood side by side there. In fact, aside from the post office and the handful of restaurants and banks, the entire district was filled with the buildings the country was managed out of. All the streets were full of bureaucrats rushing to and fro in serious-looking suits.

The administrative district was also home to a few stand-alone office buildings. They appeared to be subdivisions of larger organizations, but with unremarkable names like the Construction Bureau Office of Road Work and the Ministry of Justice Administration Bureau, it was hard to draw any real conclusions.

Klaus came to a stop in front of a small three-story building: the Cabinet Office Economic Research Center.

At first glance, Thea had no idea what kind of business they might have there—

"This building is owned by the Foreign Intelligence Office."

—but Klaus offered her a quick explanation as they went inside. After informing the receptionist that he had an appointment in Room 444, he took the proffered key and headed down a dimly lit hallway.

His shoes clicked against the marble floor.

"Hey, Teach," Thea said. "What is this place? I'd like some answers, if you don't mind."

"To put it simply, it's a prison," Klaus replied briefly. "This is where the Foreign Intelligence Office holds the spies it's captured."

The echo from his footsteps changed. The floor sounded almost hollow. Klaus tapped his foot rhythmically against the ground, and it slid away to reveal a hidden staircase.

"I figured it would be best if you saw him for yourself."

Klaus descended the staircase, and Thea followed after him with bated breath. She couldn't tell how the entrance worked, but as soon as she went down, it closed behind them.

Much to her surprise, the construction below was actually quite modern. Aside from its lack of windows, it was no different from any other facility one might visit. A wine-red carpet decorated the floor under the hallway's blaring light.

They passed by a number of cells, but Thea wasn't able to see into any of them. All she heard was sobbing and the occasional scream.

Her breath got caught in her throat.

The world was awash in pain.

Right and wrong didn't have anything to do with it. This was just the cruel reality they lived in.

Klaus came to a stop in front of one of the rooms and unlocked it without so much as hesitating. The door loudly swung open.

Inside, it was a classic solitary confinement cell. There was a bed, a toilet, and nothing else.

For a moment, it reminded her of her own time in captivity, and she gasped. She didn't want to stay there any longer than necessary.

A single man sat atop the bed.

"Hey there, Bonfire. Never thought I'd see *you* walking through that door."

Thea's eyes went wide. "Wh—?"

She recognized the man. In fact, she had faced him just the other day, and the two of them had tried to kill each other.

He was a Galgad spy—and a skilled, ruthless assassin.

In the Republic, they called him Corpse.

"I've been dying to see you. If they sent in someone weak, I might've had to kill 'em."

The man's eyes practically protruded from his skull. Klaus glared at him.

Corpse had been creepily gaunt to begin with, and his days in captivity had done a number on what little body fat he'd had. He looked like he was made of nothing more than skin and bones.

"Corpse," Klaus said. "Or Deepwater, I suppose. I guess that's what they called you in the Empire."

"Roland." The man smiled. "Please call me Roland. It's what I'm most used to."

"Alternatively, I could just not call you anything at all."

"So rude. We have a bond forged in each other's blood, and this is the treatment I get?"

The man—Roland—grinned in amusement.

For all his counterpart's good cheer, however, Klaus's expression was

as steely as could be. "You put two of our torturers in the hospital. And for no good reason."

"They left the restraints too loose. I swear, it was like amateur hour," Roland said. He didn't sound remorseful in the slightest. "And besides, I had a perfectly good reason."

"And what was that?"

"It let me see you, didn't it?"

Roland rose to his feet. As he did, he began gnawing his fingernails until they were as sharp as knives.

"C'mon, Bonfire, let's have another go. One-on-one. To the death. You won't catch me off guard this time."

"I don't have time for this," Klaus replied curtly.

"Oh, really? Well then, in that case—" Roland smirked. "—I guess I'll just have to kill the girl."

Out of nowhere, his body appeared to float in the air. That was just how blisteringly efficient his leap was. It begged the question, where in his haggard body did he find the muscles to pull off such a feat? He kicked off the wall for momentum, dove straight past Klaus, and reached for Thea's throat. The speed he was moving at was downright inhuman.

Then, the moment before his jagged nails could reach Thea's carotid artery...he froze in midair.

Klaus's fist sat buried in Roland's solar plexus.

For a moment, Roland hung there, motionless. Then he went flying and slammed into the wall with a terrible crunch.

Klaus shook his fist to loosen it back up. "That didn't even make for decent sport."

The fight had played out from start to finish before Thea even had a chance to react. And apparently, Klaus had won decisively.

"You lost, Roland. Your only job now is to spill your guts."

"Urgh..."

"I'm led to believe that there's a member of Serpent who's infiltrated the city of Mitario in the United States and is interfering with the Tolfa Economic Conference. Is that all true?"

Roland lay on the floor and groaned.

Eventually, he gave his miserable reply. "...Yeah. I was helping him out."

"Where exactly is he hiding? How can we identify him?"

"If I've told you once, I've told you a thousand times." Roland gritted his teeth and glared at Klaus. "Let me out, and I'll tell you whatever you wanna know."

Klaus looked coolly at him. "Do you really think you're in a position to be making demands?"

Roland spit on the ground in pain, plopped himself down on the bed, and sighed. Then he took the glass lying beside the bed and guzzled down the water. By the time the glass was empty, he'd regained his composure. "I mean, what else are you gonna do? Go in blind?"

"Your concern is touching, it really is."

"Sorry, man, but there's no torture or truth serum that can break me. And if you do go in there blind…"

Roland's lips curled into a mocking sneer.

"…Purple Ant will butcher every last one of you."

Purple Ant. So that was the name of the Serpent member lurking in Mitario.

However, knowing a spy's code name wasn't nearly enough to come up with a strategy to beat them.

None of that seemed to be news to Klaus, and his expression didn't change in the slightest. He merely gave Roland a frosty look. "Spare me the hollow threats."

"Oh, that wasn't a threat." Roland sounded almost proud. "Serpent already killed one of your teammates, right? If I remember correctly, they delivered the corpse right here to Din with its heart gouged out and no return address."

"………"

"Here's a prophecy for you. You're gonna lose people you care about again."

His voice rang with conviction. It was almost as though he had evidence with which to back up his claim.

Fear and unease ran through Thea's heart, and she was seized by an urge to ask Klaus to hear Roland out. She knew he was trying to tempt her. She knew that reaction was exactly what their foe was looking for. But the urge seized her all the same.

However, Klaus looked utterly unperturbed. He turned to leave. "I can see I'm wasting my time here."

Thea could hear Roland click his tongue in annoyance.

Listening to their exchange had made for a rather disconcerting experience. Thea turned toward the exit as well. She wanted to get out of there as fast as humanly possible.

When she did, though, Roland spoke to them in a grave tone. "Your loss. But hey, I'll give you one freebie," he said. "You should drop that black-haired girl from your team ASAP."

Thea stopped in her tracks with a gasp.

She could see the ridicule in Roland's smile.

"Back when I fought her, she accomplished exactly jack shit. All she did was quiver in her boots and run for her life. If I were you, I'd get rid of her before she drags you down with her."

Thea felt her entire body go hot.

It was all true. Back when she'd faced off against him, she had been able to do nothing. Her teammate Monika had fought back against him just fine, but Thea had completely given in to her weakness.

Even now, she wanted to flee as fast as she could, but—

"Interesting. I actually had something I wanted to ask, too."

Klaus turned back. The look in his eyes was still as cold as ice.

"What was it? What was it that compelled a two-bit weakling like you to think of me as your rival?"

"………"

This time, it was Roland's turn to look shaken.

"It must be pretty embarrassing for you, all that nonsense you believed about 'fate bringing us together' and 'lifelong rivalries.' Whose bullshit have you been listening to? Know your place—your life as a spy is over."

With those merciless final words, Klaus left the cell.

As Thea followed after him, she stole a glance back at Roland.

His face was bright red, and he pounded the wall in frustration.

After they came up from the basement, Klaus called over to her. "I'm sorry about that."

It was unusual, hearing him apologize.

"You're going to be taking command during the mission, so I thought it would be best for you to see firsthand who our intel was coming from. I had no intention of putting you in harm's way, and I had no idea he would make those baseless comments about you."

Thea shook her head. "No, no, it's not your fault..."

She understood where he'd been coming from. Their whole mission had come about because of "Corpse" Roland's testimony. She was glad that Klaus had gone out of his way to let her be present as he confirmed the details.

However...she was at her limit.

Her heart was coming apart at the seams.

"Teach." She called out to him from behind. "Everything Roland said was true. I was too scared to contribute."

"I see."

"Are you really sure I'm qualified to act as CO?"

It was a pathetic thing to ask. She knew that. But she asked it anyway.

Having to give orders with her teammates' lives on the line was a heavy responsibility to bear, and she wasn't sure her heart could handle that weight.

The lighting was dim, so she couldn't see Klaus's expression. She wondered just how disappointed he looked as she clutched at her chest and went on. "I...I helped an enemy spy get away once."

"........."

"It wasn't a mistake or an accident, either. I gave instructions to my teammates and had them save one of our enemies."

Klaus nodded like he'd already known. "I see."

Thea was talking about what had happened a few days ago.

She and the others had met Matilda, a woman claiming to be Annette's mother, and when they found out that Matilda was an enemy spy, Thea had made the call to help her get away. Some of her allies had objected, but she'd won them over and forced them to handle things the way she thought was right.

However, there was a good chance that it had all been part of their enemy's plan.

"*Thea, honey, you're a nobody.*"

Thea would never forget the scornful look in Matilda's eyes.

"It made me realize something... That I'm too soft on my enemies."

She thought back to her idol's words.

It had all started because of something the spy Hearth had said to her. *"I want you to become a hero."*

Those words were the reason she'd become a spy in the first place, but now, they felt like a curse weighing her down.

Unlike spies who saved only their countrymen, heroes saved their enemies, too. Now, though, she realized what a fantasy that ideal of hers was. If she kept letting her softness control her, all it was going to do was put her teammates in peril.

"I'm not cut out for commanding. Everyone would be better off with you back at the helm, the way you were before."

It was too big a burden for her.

And besides, Klaus had taken command during their first Impossible Mission, hadn't he? She and the others had drawn up the plan and taken care of relaying intel to him, but he was the one who'd had the final say-so on everything. Why couldn't he just do that again?

However, Klaus just sighed. "I can't sign off on that."

"But why not?"

"Because we don't know enough about who it is we're up against. With so little information to work off, the only way we can learn about our foe is by fumbling around blindly. That means extra danger for the people on the front lines, which is why one of them needs to be me."

".........."

Thea had no rebuttal to that. It was a rational decision.

Sure enough, they had succeeded in gathering advance intel on all their other opponents to date. Whether they'd been going up against Klaus's mentor or against someone their fellow compatriots had laid down their lives to investigate, they had always been able to prepare countermeasures.

This time, though, things were different.

Who other than Klaus could they possibly put in charge of life-threatening reconnaissance?

"Don't beat yourself up so hard," Klaus said gently. "Remember what I told you? Differences between allies are the key to a strong team. Ruthlessness may have served the team well in the past, but the day will come when that empathy of yours is exactly what we need."

When, though?

How many times will I have to get hurt while I wait?

And what if my naivete costs us one of our teammates before then?

She wanted to shout questions at him like a child, but Klaus had already left the building and hailed a taxi. Now that they were in public, she couldn't talk about work anymore.

The two of them got in the back seat, and the taxi took off.

"Once we get to the station, why don't we stop for lunch?" Klaus suggested. "It'll help get you out of your head."

The kindness was uncharacteristic, coming from him.

A lot of the time, he was actually pretty cold to her, and on occasion, she could hear something like disgust in his voice. Now, though, all she heard in it was sympathy.

"Teach...could you comfort me?" The words escaped her almost involuntarily. "Will you promise not to abandon me for being worthless...?"

"Of course," Klaus responded instantly. "Looking out for my subordinates' mental well-being is part of the job, so I—"

She grabbed him by the arm. "Thank you. Let's head to a hotel and make love, then."

Klaus's voice went very cold very fast. "What are you on about? Need I remind you we're in a taxi?"

Thea glared at him. She felt a little betrayed. "You're awful. You just said you would comfort me!"

"I was talking about taking you to a nice restaurant."

"Oh, no, don't worry. I'll call Grete and have her join us at the hotel."

"You're taking years off my life here." Klaus massaged his temples. "I swear, sometimes you're more of a headache than Lily is." It was a pretty rude comment, to say nothing of the fact that it implied Lily was the benchmark he used to judge how annoying things were.

However, Thea refused to back down.

This is the only way I know how to get rid of gloomy feelings...

Klaus had agreed to comfort her, and she intended to make him honor that. This time, it would take more than a few thoughtful words to satisfy her.

She called up to the front seat. "Driver, could you take that right up ahead? There's a hotel I've been wanting to visit for ages. I hear they have waterslides right in the rooms."

She chose to ignore the way Klaus was scowling at her.

However, the taxi went straight through the intersection where she'd wanted to turn.

"Ah, I guess I needed to speak up sooner." She collected herself, then made another request. "In that case, could you take this next right instead? The fanciest hotel in the area is nearby. They have huge bathtubs there that light up in all the colors of the rainbow."

"Your depth of knowledge on the subject is a little concerning," Klaus commented, but Thea continued ignoring him. He wasn't getting out of this. She was prepared to check the whole taxi into the hotel if she had to.

Yet, once again, the taxi barreled straight past the turn.

Now Thea was starting to get suspicious. Why was their driver so determined to continue going straight? And was she just imagining things, or were they going *really* fast?

"I-I'm so sorry, ma'am."

Thea looked up into the front seats and discovered that their driver, a mature-looking woman in her late thirties, was as pale as a sheet.

"I—I think there's something wrong with my car," the driver said, her voice trembling.

The fear in her expression was all too plain to see.

"It's doing forty miles an hour, and I can't make it slow down."

As Thea stared at their driver in shock, Klaus acted fast.

With a brief "pardon me," he grabbed the woman by the nape of her neck and pulled her into the back of the cab. As he did, he hopped forward and took her spot in the driver's seat.

Once situated, he grabbed hold of the wheel and quickly inspected the state of the taxi. "The brakes don't work, it keeps going even with my foot off the gas, and the parking brake doesn't do anything, either... This is no run-of-the-mill breakdown." Klaus shot a glance at the passenger seat, then used the rearview mirror to look at the driver. "Has anything unusual happened to you these last few days?"

"Anything...unusual?" The woman averted her eyes. "That's, um, well..."

"I can guess. Someone got ahold of some compromising information, and they've been using it to blackmail you. Is that about right?"

"H-how can you know that?"

"I just do. Now hurry up and tell me what happened."

The woman's gaze darted around in bewilderment, but she eventually began quietly explaining. "I—I was embezzling. Every now and then, I stole money from the safe in our office. But then this bearded man showed up and told me that he knew what I'd done. I had no choice but to do as he said…"

"And what was that?"

"He wanted me to give you two a ride in my taxi."

They had fallen right into their foe's trap.

"Ah," Klaus replied with a small nod. "I have a pretty good idea of what's happening. I do apologize for how you got dragged into our mess, but at the end of the day, you brought this on yourself. I would recommend thinking long and hard about the choices you've made."

"I know…"

Still using one hand to hold the steering wheel, Klaus scrawled something on the taxi's memo pad and handed it to the woman.

"Once this is over, call this number. They'll compensate you for the inconvenience. You should use this as an opportunity to get your life together."

"Wh-who are you people…?"

"That's none of your concern. I need you to close your eyes and cover your ears. I promise nothing will happen to you."

The woman took the memo pad, then did as Klaus said, clamping her hands over her ears and hanging her head.

All the while, the taxi continued speeding through the city at a forty-mile-an-hour clip. Turning would be a challenge, and while they were good to continue on forward for a little while more, they would eventually come to a red light. When that happened, it all but assured they would crash into someone. Everything rested on Klaus's driving skills.

Thea shrieked at the impending danger. "T-Teach, what's going on? Why are we—?"

"You've gotten good at staying hidden." Klaus gave the passenger seat a thump. "I take it we have you to thank for this, Annette?"

When he did, the seat bulged, and a young head popped up like it had just gnawed itself free from beneath.

"You found me, yo!"

It was Annette.

Nothing below her neck was visible; it looked as though the seat itself had sprouted a head. There was no knowing what sorts of drastic modifications she'd made to the taxi.

"B-but why?" Thea asked.

"Lily gave me a message to pass on," the disembodied Annette head said. "'Teach, if you want the taxi to stop, all you have to do is acknowledge your defeat.'"

Upon hearing that, Thea finally realized what was going on.

It was a training exercise—the same one the girls always did, where they tried to get Klaus to say, *I surrender.*

Klaus gave Lily's offer a flat "that's not going to happen."

"I assume you're gonna say no, so this is where I'd like to explain what's going on, but…I figure you get the drill by now. Still, we put in even more effort than usual this time. The big mission is right around the corner, so we decided to get seriouser than serious! It's time for you to see just how much we've grown during our domestic missions!"

It appeared that that was the end of the message. Annette clamped her mouth shut.

Once she was finished, Klaus seemed pleased. "Magnificent."

They plowed right through a red light and were greeted by a cacophony of honks as they continued down the thoroughfare. They were one tiny misstep away from getting into a huge crash, but Klaus didn't look the least bit afraid.

"You know, I was just thinking that I wanted to see how far you all had come. This works out perfectly."

If anything, he seemed to be enjoying himself.

Thea could see that he was planning on rising to the challenge. She would have felt a lot more comfortable if he'd just surrendered immediately, but alas.

Upon hearing that, Annette wriggled herself free from within the passenger seat. She was wearing a large bag strapped on her back; by the look of it, it was some sort of airbag.

She headed to the back seat and grabbed the driver by her collar. "Annette out, yo!"

Apparently, her plan was to escape with the woman in tow.

"Wait, Annette, what about me?" Thea asked in a panic.

"The airbag only supports two," Annette replied cheerily. "Sis, your job's to be the hostage. Do what you can to get in his way, 'kay?"

"Wh—?"

"And a hip, hop, and away we go!"

Annette pressed a button on the remote control she was holding, and the taxi's door popped open. She took the driver and leaped from the speeding vehicle. Her airbag opened in midair, and the two of them bounced off the ground before rolling to a stop by the side of the road.

Now Thea and Klaus were alone in a runaway car.

Thea finally grasped the full situation.

Those dastardly teammates of hers had chosen a gambit that put *her* life in danger, too!

"Is it just me, or did I get stuck with the *worst* role?" She hurriedly fastened her seat belt, then shouted up to the front. "T-Teach, you have to stop the taxi, quick! You know a way to, right?"

"I do, but it would leave me vulnerable in the moments just afterward." Klaus was totally calm. "This is Annette we're dealing with. I imagine she has the car set to blow up the moment it stops."

"I want to get off this wild ride!"

"For the time being, I'm going to get us out of the city. I'll stop the car once we're out of their transmitter's range."

With that, Klaus yanked the steering wheel hard to the side.

Still traveling at breakneck speeds, the taxi skidded sideways down the road. That caused them to slow down a bit, but the gas pedal quickly pressed itself into the floor and started speeding them back up. It hadn't been pretty, but they'd successfully made a left turn. A passing truck very nearly flattened them, but the taxi accelerated just in time, and they began heading toward the mountains.

Klaus gave a little nod. He'd figured out how to turn—and in stunning form. "It's odd," he murmured. "Why just forty miles per hour? I'm sure she wouldn't have had a problem making it go faster than that."

"Oh, I can think of a couple problems!"

"At forty, making that left turn was perfectly easy."

"For you, maybe."

Still, it was a legitimate question.

If they had *really* wanted to keep Klaus pinned down, they would've needed to jack the taxi up to 120 miles per hour. At least, Thea assumed they would've.

"Could it be that they kept the speed down because they didn't want to risk actually causing a serious accident?"

"That's a possibility. What else could it be?"

"Maybe it was out of compassion? As in, they didn't want to hurt you?"

"Do those seven have a compassionate bone in their bodies?"

"........."

They did not.

Even Grete, who held a great deal of affection toward Klaus, was utterly merciless when it came to their training. "If we beat him, we'll be able to force the boss to rest," she'd once earnestly explained.

What other reason could they have had, though?

The answer to that question became clear once they made their way out of the city and began heading across the mountain roads.

"Ah. The bird," Klaus muttered quietly.

On hearing him, Thea stuck her head out the window and spotted the chubby pigeon soaring across the sky. It was flying directly above them. That was why they hadn't noticed it—a taxi's roof was opaque, so it was hard for the people inside them to look straight up.

"We weren't dealing with a transmitter at all," Klaus noted. "Sara sent one of her pets to tail the taxi."

"Oh, and forty miles per hour is slow enough for a pigeon to keep up with..."

By using the pigeon as a landmark, the rest of the team was able to track Klaus's location with ease. It was an ingenious little trick.

Then they spotted Sara standing on the roof of a nearby house. She turned toward Klaus down in the driver's seat and grinned.

I've got my eye on you. You'll never get away, she mouthed triumphantly.

She probably would have used her hawk Bernard, but he was still recuperating from his injuries. The road became more and more mountainous, but the pigeon continued diligently tracking them. It was impressive, both in terms of speed and stamina. He normally worked as a carrier pigeon, but he was filling Bernard's shoes with aplomb. As Thea recalled, his name was Aiden.

"Now it comes down to who can better predict the other," Klaus remarked once they had left the residential area behind them. "The question is, where am I going to stop the car? They know exactly where I am, so I'm sure they've circled ahead and are planning on jumping me the moment I stop."

"I—I vote we optimize for *safety* here."

"Just up ahead, there's a big curve in the road surrounded by woods. Once we make it there, I can use the curve to send us into a tailspin and stop the car by crashing us into a tree—"

"That doesn't sound safe at all!"

"—but the problem there is *her*."

When Thea looked around, she discovered that the mountain road was a single lane flanked on both sides by a dense forest of evergreen trees. Visibility there was terrible.

Yet even still, the taxi refused to drop below forty miles per hour.

Sure enough, hitting the trees at that speed was a recipe for disaster. Their only option was to do as Klaus said and wait for the curve where the road would be wider.

Klaus frowned. "And there she is. Thea, in five seconds, we're going to jump out of the back-right door."

"What?!"

"It'll leave me pretty vulnerable, but there's no two ways about it. This taxi is going to flip over."

It all seemed horribly abrupt.

Before she had a chance to process what she'd just been told, Thea saw something.

"Only she could leap out in front of a car that's about to crash."

Someone had just appeared in the middle of the road like a fell specter. It was Erna.

Her lips twitched ominously. "How unlucky..."

It was like looking at the Grim Reaper.

Klaus immediately yanked the steering wheel to the side. Unable to change course so abruptly, the taxi tilted hard to the left. Its right wheels practically grazed the side of Erna's head as they passed her by.

Erna had found the location precisely in front of where the accident was going to take place and positioned herself on the road at exactly that spot. It was a feat that only she, as someone who'd spent her life constantly brushing up against disaster, could pull off.

Just as the taxi was about to flip over, Thea felt Klaus's arm wrapped around her. As the taxi tilted to the left, he dashed up the back seat and escaped out the right rear door.

After they escaped, the taxi did a barrel roll.

Klaus continued holding Thea tightly as they tumbled to the ground. Fortunately, he managed to blunt the impact. They rolled across the ground a few times but were otherwise fine. The fact that he had gotten them out of the car unharmed was nothing short of astounding.

However, his opponents weren't about to waste the opening he'd just given them.

"Here they come."

And sure enough, the moment the words left Klaus's mouth—

"Brace yourself!"

—Lily burst out from behind a tree. She approached Klaus with her gun at the ready and fired it without a moment's hesitation.

Klaus didn't miss a beat. He brandished a knife and swatted her bullet out of the air.

However, that fell well within Lily's expectations. The bullet was little more than a diversion to let her approach him. Once she was closer, her true objective came to light.

A smoke screen billowed out from her chest.

Klaus immediately fell back to evade the smoke, and though Thea tried to do the same thing a moment later, the delay caused her to breathe in a small mouthful. Her body went numb. That was no ordinary smoke screen; it was Lily's special-made poison gas.

Thea collapsed onto the ground, helpless to do anything but watch.

Then Sybilla charged straight through the smoke.

With a dauntless smile, she launched a series of gorgeous high kicks at Klaus's head.

"Looks like your injury's all better." Klaus nodded as he blocked her blows. "Good, that means I can get a bit rough."

"Ha! Do your wor—" Sybilla's voice cut out mid-taunt.

Klaus had launched a swift elbow strike at her flank. However, Sybilla reacted fast. She pulled her arm down to block Klaus's masterful attack.

Her resistance didn't last long.

Klaus's next attack was a palm strike to her jaw, and this time, she was launched into the air.

By all accounts, it appeared she was no match for him in a fight, but...

"You might've gotten me..." A smile played at Sybilla's lips. "But check out what I just nicked."

Clutched in her right hand was Klaus's knife.

As she crumpled to the ground, she let out a shout. "Go show him why they call you our ace in the hole!"

An airy "don't mind if I do" cut through the smoke, followed immediately by another Lamplight member—Monika.

She fired at Klaus from point-blank range.

Klaus had no tool with which to swat down the bullets anymore. He twisted his body to the side to dodge, but while he was still mid-rotation, Monika bore down on him with a roundhouse kick.

Then she let out a groan. "Agh!"

"You were a little too slow there," Klaus said.

Thea stared in stark disbelief at the high-speed back-and-forth going on before her.

The combo attack Lily, Sybilla, and Monika had just executed was far more polished than anything they'd managed before. If their timing had been even the slightest bit off, Sybilla and Monika would've gotten big mouthfuls of poison gas, but if either of them had hesitated before diving through the smoke screen, it would have given Klaus time to collect himself.

The Operations squad's teamwork had truly come far.

However, they were still no match for Klaus.

"We couldn't beat him, even with three people attacking in waves...?" Thea moaned.

Suddenly, she heard an arrogant voice.

"That's why we sent four."

One more figure rushed out of the fumes.

"You're wide open, Klaus."

Before anyone knew it, the figure was directly behind Klaus. And the figure was a second Monika.

She'd completely gotten the drop on him.

Not only had she shown up behind him, she'd done so at a speed that put the first Monika to shame. She pressed her trusty revolver against his shoulder.

For a moment, time seemed to freeze.

That was checkmate.

Klaus stopped moving and raised his hands in the air. Behind him, Monika set her finger on the trigger.

"It's over," she said.

".........."

Klaus was silent.

Thea couldn't believe her eyes. Monika's gun was flush with Klaus's body. If he moved an inch, she would shoot.

At that point, it all sank in—this was real.

We finally won? We beat Teach…?

Thea's eyes went wide.

They had gone after Klaus more than a hundred times, but out of all those attempts, this was the first time they'd ever been able to back him into a corner like this.

A gust of wind blew, clearing up the smoke screen that obscured the roadway.

At some point, the rest of Lamplight had arrived as well.

Annette, Sara, Erna, Lily, Sybilla, Monika, and the second Monika were all there, pointing their guns at Klaus with bated breath.

"Ah." Klaus nodded. "So the first Monika was Grete in disguise."

"That's right…"

The first Monika reached up and pulled off her mask.

Beneath it was Grete, Lamplight's strategist and resident master of disguise.

"…Just as I expected. Even you would have to put up your guard when you saw Monika, Boss. I thought we could use that to create an opening."

Everything had gone according to plan.

Nobody but Grete could have possibly seen how things would play out in such exacting detail, and on top of that, the girls' teamwork was incredible. Grete was probably the one who'd blackmailed the taxi driver, and she had represented the Intel squad and set the team into motion. From there, the Specialist squad laid the groundwork to ensnare Klaus, and once their trap was sprung, the Operations squad trio had jumped in at the perfect time.

None of it would have been possible if not for the experience they'd built up during their domestic missions.

"All right, Klaus. Time's a-wasting." Monika smiled sadistically. "Can we get that *I surrender*? If you don't hurry it up, my finger might just slip."

".........." Klaus hadn't said anything for a little while.

He wasn't putting up any resistance. Even if he tried to pull anything, Monika would be faster on the draw. He was well and truly bested.

Klaus let out a big exhale. "Magnificent."

Then he lowered his raised hands and clapped. The look in his eyes softened a bit. This wasn't sarcastic, condescending applause. He was giving them an honest-to-goodness round of congratulations.

"You did brilliantly. The one warning I would give you is that in the position I'm in, a first-rate spy could still put up a fight if they were prepared to suffer a few injuries. That said, I obviously can't afford to get injured right now. I won't be putting up a fight."

"——!"

Hearing that came as a shock to the girls.

Normally, Klaus would use his spy techniques to turn the tables on them right when they were sure they had him cornered. This time, though, he wasn't doing a thing.

His face was lit up with uncharacteristic joy.

"You've worked hard, and you've become strong. I told you you had boundless potential just waiting to be unlocked."

He gently cast his gaze around the group.

"Annette. The way you rigged the taxi was fantastic, but the thing that impressed me most of all was the way you hid yourself so undetectably in its frame. I'm counting on you to use that out-of-the-box intuition of yours to help out the team."

"If that's an order, Bro, then you got it," Annette replied happily. She did a little hop in the air.

"Sara. The way you coordinated with your animals was as impeccable as always. Try to be a little more confident in yourself. Aside from just your skills, your kindness is an unmistakable asset in a team as full of oddballs as ours."

"I-I'll try," Sara said nervously.

"Erna. That special skill of yours really is unique, and nobody can lead their enemies around by the nose quite the way you can. The future will doubtless hold more hardships for you, but I know you'll be able to overcome them."

Erna looked totally composed. "With you by my side, I'm not afraid of anything."

Once he was done speaking to the team's younger members, Klaus turned his gaze to the Operations squad. "Lily, Sybilla, Monika. You three are the cornerstone of this team. Watching you charge valiantly into danger gives the others the courage they need to do their best, and while you get carried away sometimes, it's that same confidence that lets you draw out everything you have."

Lily threw out her chest. "Yup! Leave it all to Wunderkind Lily!"

Sybilla responded in much the same way. "Yeah, you can count on us."

"Please don't lump me in with Tweedledumb and Tweedledumber," Monika sullenly grumbled.

Klaus turned toward the next girl. "Grete. As for you, I—"

"It's okay, Boss, you don't have to say it. You've shown me exactly how you feel," Grete said, shaking her head. "I have the marriage registration all ready for you to sign."

"Um, no."

"...Boo."

"During the Corpse mission, your skills advanced by leaps and bounds. Together with Monika, the two of you are already at the point where you could go toe to toe against most elite spies. During this upcoming mission, I ask that you use that ingenuity of yours to its fullest extent."

Grete bowed respectfully. "It's an honor to hear you say that, Boss."

"Don't call me 'Boss,'" Klaus quickly corrected her.

Then, he turned to the team's final member.

"Thea."

"Y-yes? What is it?"

"Given the slump you're in, I imagine any words of encouragement

I offered you would only make you feel worse. Just remember this—
you have teammates you can rely on."

"........."

She couldn't come up with a good reply to that.

However, his thoughtfulness had come across loud and clear.

A soft mood fell over them, and Monika laughed teasingly. "What,
are you about to start handing out diplomas or something?"

The rest of the girls followed her lead and grinned.

It really did feel sort of like a graduation ceremony, and the girls'
expressions looked touched and embarrassed in equal measure. They
were all proud of the hard-won compliments they'd just received from
their instructor.

Klaus didn't deny it. "Maybe I should. As I recall, your graduations
are merely provisional. You all still have some individual problems to
work out, but the explosive power you've shown while working in
coordinated unison is easily worthy of graduate status. Why don't we
call this next mission your graduation exam? Once you complete it,
you'll all be full-fledged spies."

A cheer rose up from the girls. "Woo-hoo!"

It was an issue that had been plaguing them for ages.

All of them still bore the brand of "spy academy washout." Not only
had they failed to graduate, but they had each been right on the verge
of flunking out altogether. Getting recruited into Lamplight had let
them skip some steps and get right to clearing missions, but deep in their
hearts, they couldn't shake the feeling that they were still amateurs.

The prospect of finally graduating was downright scintillating. They
couldn't help but clench their fists in excitement.

"Sorry to be a buzzkill, but I don't care one bit about all that." There
was just one member who wasn't rejoicing, and it was Monika. "More
importantly, I want to hear that *I surrender*. Don't go thinking you can
cheat us out of it."

"What a very Monika thing to say," Klaus replied.

"Look, it's pretty obvious I'm good enough to graduate already. My
desire to take you down is a hundred times more important than any
of that stuff."

Monika was a prideful person, and it was clear that she'd built up a sizable grudge. During their whole exchange, she'd been grinding her revolver into Klaus's shoulder.

"You have a point, though," he replied. "I suppose I should go ahead and hand down the verdict."

"Yeah. And loud enough so everyone can hear, if you don't mind."

"Very well."

With that, Klaus raised his hands into the air once more.

It was the universally recognized pose that signified nonresistant surrender.

Monika flashed him her pearly whites. "Seeing's great and all, but I want to *hear* it."

"Of course. Oh, and by the way…," Klaus said.

"…how much longer should I keep playing along with this game?"

The sound of sirens split the air.

Thea's eyes went wide as she checked to see what was going on. Those were, without a doubt, police sirens. And they were closing in from both sides of the road.

"Cops?" Monika clicked her tongue. "The hell's going on? When we blackmailed that driver, we warned her not to go to the police."

Thea couldn't believe it, either.

Klaus had been forced to spend all his attention keeping the taxi under control, so he'd never had the time to call in a report. And as for the taxi driver, the others had gotten her under control by threatening to expose her embezzlement.

So why were the police on their way?

"You did a poor job of choosing your mark. It was a good idea on paper, but you should never have used a woman that loose-lipped. She told me all about the embezzlement."

"___!"

"All I had to do was blackmail her the same way you did. 'I'll keep quiet about what you did, but in exchange, I need you to call the police for me,' I told her."

It wasn't hard for Thea to figure out when he'd delivered the threat. *It was on that memo he wrote…!*

During the ride, Klaus had handed a memo pad to the driver. He must have secretly written the instructions on the note. He'd even predicted where the girls would stage their attack and included the location, too.

From the woman's perspective, Klaus was a man who'd risked his own life to take over for her in a runaway taxi. She might have even become a bit smitten with him.

"You should get out of here while you can. After all, what do you imagine the cops will think? I doubt they'll look kindly on you all for holding a fine, upstanding citizen such as myself at gunpoint."

"...Tch," Monika replied. "If this were a real fight, I'd shoot you right here and now."

"And if you did, I would fight back—long enough for the police to get here and arrest you."

Monika bit her lip in frustration at Klaus's rebuttal.

The thing was, their failure to make him say *I surrender*—or to put it in terms of an actual battle, to make him give up the information they needed—meant that they had lost.

The siren noises drew closer.

"L-let's book it! Retreat, retreat!" Lily cried. She rushed off into the woods, and the others followed along after her.

Thea merely stared at them until Sybilla yanked her to her feet. "Quit futzin' around—we gotta go!" she shouted as she dragged Thea along.

There was no particular reason for Thea to have to escape, but she chose to obediently follow along anyway. Lily's poison had long since worn off.

"Ah, right. Thea," Klaus called after her as she moved to leave. "I'm going to be taking the next three days off to rest and prepare for the mission, so I won't be coming back to Heat Haze Palace. Do keep an eye on the others for me, won't you?"

"W-will do."

For the time being, their training with Klaus would be on pause. He was going to tackle the mission with everything he had right alongside them.

Thea dashed through the forest with the rest of the team.

After running for a little while, they arrived at the automobile her teammates had stashed away in advance. They explained to her that they had stolen it from a gang, then remodeled it and given it a fresh coat of paint to make it into a whole new car. Say what you will about them, they never did anything by half measures.

The car itself was a foreign-made V16 with quite a few miles on it, and its ivory black body gleamed in the light. It was also on the larger size, so it seated six.

Once they were sure they were safe, the girls broke into smiles.

"Ah, what a bummer. And we were so close, too," Lily said.

"Really? Feels to me like we haven't shrunk the gap one damn bit," Sybilla replied. Her voice rang with exasperation.

"No, no, really! He said we were worthy of graduate status, didn't he?"

"I mean, he *did*, but...it kinda felt like he was saying that with *all eight of us together*, we were *only just barely* on par with a full-fledged spy."

"Hey, full-fledged is full-fledged!"

"Always the optimist, ain'tcha? But yeah, hey, I guess that's still somethin' worth celebrating."

"Right? Now let's go finish that mission and win our graduations!"

For all their good cheer, though, Thea couldn't bring herself to join in.

"........."

What they'd achieved was fantastic, make no mistake. Thea had watched the whole thing play out, and for a moment, she really thought they'd had him.

But the thing was...they had done it without her.

The rest of the team was making all that progress, and she hadn't been part of any of it.

"Y'know," Lily murmured, "if we'd had Thea with us, we might've actually won."

Upon being asked, she explained herself with a smile.

"Our big mistake this time around was how our stooge betrayed us, right? If Thea had been on board, I bet she could've done a way better job negotiating with her."

"........."

For a moment, Thea's heart leaped at Lily's kind words, but a moment later, reality came crashing back down on her.

I can't. If I get my hopes up, I'll just make a fool of myself again. They didn't need me for their plan, and that's the cold hard truth.

Her being there wouldn't have changed a thing.

Klaus would simply have chosen some other method, and he would have trounced them all the same.

"You made the right call, not telling me about the plan. If I had known anything, Teach would have realized that something was up," she said, fleeing from Lily's compliment before slumping down in the back seat. The rest of the girls piled in, and though they immediately started up their post-mortem discussion, Thea couldn't bring herself to take part.

Even after they set off, all she did was stare out the window.

It's like I can feel my heart breaking apart...

She could see her reflection in the window overlaid atop the scenery, and her expression was clouded with gloom. She stuck out like a sore thumb. The other three girls in the back seat and the two in the passenger seat were all sunny smiles, and yet she alone was—

Suddenly, she realized something.

"Wait, doesn't this car only seat six? We don't have enough room!"

They had too many people. With only six seats, there weren't enough to go around.

The rest of the team was feeling cramped as well, and they made their pained complaints one after another.

"Yeah, I can barely breathe," Monika grumbled. "I'm getting off when we reach the end of this road. God, I'm still pissed..."

"Wait, hold up," Sara said. "Where's Miss Annette?"

"I'm clinging to the roof, yo."

"Please come down," Grete responded. "It isn't safe up there. Lily, can you find somewhere to pull over?"

"Who, me? I'm not driving. I'm in the passenger seat."

"My legs only barely reach the pedals...," Erna said. "B-but! I'm doing my best!"

"You're the last damn person I want driving *anything*!" Sybilla cried.

And so they clamored on, oblivious to Thea's heartache.

As Klaus watched the girls go, something about them seemed almost radiant to him.

He leaned against the overturned taxi and caught his breath. Their attack this time around had been even more extreme than usual. Between the guns and the runaway car, he could tell they hadn't pulled any punches. They had been careful to toe the line and avoid seriously injuring him, but aside from that, there was little difference between what they'd just done and the kind of effort they put into real fights.

These training exercises are getting dangerously close to actual life-and-death battles, but...I suppose this is a special occasion.

Klaus decided to take it as a good thing that they were so fired up about their mission in the United States. He was impressed at how motivated they all were. To be totally honest, it had kind of caught him by surprise.

Given how dangerous this mission will be, I was expecting them to be a little more nervous.

It wasn't to say that they were totally unafraid, of course. Some of their courage was just for show, and many of them probably had worries they were merely keeping to themselves.

Still, they were overcoming all that.

That's Lily's influence at work, no doubt.

Her espionage skill may have been lacking, but she always played a huge role in keeping the team's spirits high.

Nobody else had quite the same cheer and indomitable mental fortitude she did. Her acting and her poison were one thing, but that was where her true talents lay.

Those were the talents that never got a chance to shine back at her academy.

I never imagined that that random title of "Leader" I gave her would end up paying so many dividends.

There was no way he'd ever admit it to her, but when he'd appointed her as team leader, he had done so on little more than a whim. On the face of things, Thea, Monika, or Grete would have been better suited to the job.

In retrospect, though, Klaus realized he had made the right call.

"I'm a little worried about Thea's lack of confidence, but I guess I just have to trust the others."

It was going to be up to Lily and the rest of the girls to lift Thea up.

The thing was, Klaus's chemistry with Thea was abysmal.

At the end of the day, their social mores were simply incompatible.

When he wanted to comfort her, he had offered her food, but what she'd wanted was sex. It was unfortunate, but there was nothing he could do for her. Thea was going to be the key to their upcoming mission, and it was up to the rest of the team to support her.

Right when Klaus finished organizing his thoughts, the patrol car pulled up. An officer got out and rushed over to him. "You're the victim of that runaway taxi, right?"

"That I am." Klaus nodded. "As you can see, I'm nothing more than a fine, upstanding citizen of our good Republic."

"Uh-huh... I must say, you've had quite a day. I hear you were attacked by terrorists. Rumors are flying all around, and between that and your fancy driving, this incident's become the talk of the town. I wonder what sort of conspiracy it was you got yourself caught up in?"

"........."

This was becoming quite the to-do.

I do wish they'd chosen a method that wouldn't cause such a commotion...

No matter how you sliced it, they had taken things too far.

The question was, how best to deal with this mess they'd left for him?

Meanwhile, the rest of Lamplight was still chattering away.

After they ousted Erna from the driver's seat, had Sybilla take over, and dragged Annette down from the roof while they were at it, the girls' conversation in the cramped car picked right back up.

Lily smiled as she sat in the passenger seat with Annette on her lap. "I'm so excited to go to the United States. Now it *totally* feels like the fate of the world rests in our hands!"

"Glad you're so upbeat about it." Sybilla laughed as she continued driving. "But yeah, aside from all the parts of me that're scared, I guess I'm kinda excited, too. I bet they've got all sorts of cool stuff over there that we don't."

"Ooh, I wonder if we'll get a chance to go sightseeing once the mission is over?"

"I dunno, but...it'd be so cool if we did. I wanna check out this 'baseball' sport they've got."

At that point, Monika spoke up from the back seat. "By the way, Sybilla, you learned their language yet?" she asked.

"*N-naistoo, m-meechoo...*"

"God, you're terrible."

"Oh, shut up! I'll study on the boat; it'll be fine!"

"That's, like, year-one stuff at the academy, though..."

Monika and Sybilla's bickering sent a wave of laughter through the car.

The other girls started piping up with their own hopes and wishes.

"I wanna watch a TV broadcast, yo. And buy up all their appliances," said Annette.

"I wouldn't mind checking out their art galleries and museums," mused Monika. "And the subways there are supposed to be super nice."

"I want to see that big famous goddess statue!" Erna said. "I hear it's amazing!"

"I want to buy up every record I can get my hands on as souvenirs. I'm a big jazz fan," offered Sara.

"...It would be nice to have a chance to go to a music hall with the boss," said Grete.

The fun daydreams just kept on coming.

There was talk of how good their hamburgers were supposed to be, of how famous such-and-such Square was, and of all sorts of other exciting things they'd read in their tourist guides. Their deadly mission wasn't the only thing they had to look forward to in that yet-untrodden land.

In the end, they decided to all take a big furlough together once the mission was complete.

"Let's do this!" Lily shouted excitedly. "United States, ahoy!"

""""""Woo-hoo!""""""

The others responded to her cheer in kind.

None of that was the point of their trip, but nobody called attention to that fact. It was like they had come to a tacit understanding—they could save all that serious stuff for later.

The only one who didn't join their happy little circle was Thea. As she sat in the car's cramped back seat, she let out a heavy sigh.

It feels like I'm the only one who's stuck at a standstill.

Her feelings of inferiority refused to fade.

The rest of the team was in peak form. Their skills were honed, and their motivation for the mission was high, and there wasn't a single worry plaguing their hearts.

Thea alone was being left behind in every aspect of both body and soul.

"........."

She had heard it over and over and over and over and over and over and over and over and over and over again—Matilda's mockery echoing in her ears like a curse.

"*Thea, honey, you're a nobody. You're too soft, and you're incredibly easy to manipulate.*"

That laughter of hers refused to fade, too.

It forced Thea to ask herself a question, and not for the first time.

What kind of spy should I try to become?

Two weeks later, after a long sea voyage, Lamplight arrived in the United States of Mouzaia.

Mitario was a global metropolis, and it was there in that city of hope and despair that their decisive battle would begin.

Interlude

Purple Ant ②

In the end, she never told him a thing about how she'd gotten to Mouzaia. All she'd done was narrow her eyes a bit, like she was thinking back through her memories. Reminiscing on a life she'd never be able to return to, no doubt.

Purple Ant observed his captive. When he said she was younger than he'd expected, he had meant every word. Given the outstanding espionage work she'd been doing in Mitario, he had assumed she would be far older and far more experienced.

She still hadn't given him her name.

However, he didn't mind. Purple Ant was perfectly happy taking it slow and leisurely thinking it over. He still had plenty of time.

He ordered another cola.

His exclusive bartender broke off some ice with his ice pick, then garnished the drink with a lemon slice before serving it to him. Purple Ant took a sip. Then, as he let it linger on his tongue, a knock echoed through the room.

"Come in," he said, and a naked man wearing a dog collar came into the bar.

"………"

His captive gave their new intruder a quizzical look.

Purple Ant smiled amiably. "You were acting rather cold, so I thought the gentlemanly thing to do would be to tell you a story myself. I imagine you're curious, after all. You want to know why it is you and your people lost to me."

Then he barked an order to the collared man. **"Sit."**

A pained look crossed the man's face for a moment, but he obediently took a seat on the ground.

"Allow me to introduce you. This is my pet dog."

"......"

"Up until five years ago, he was a med student at Mitario University. People called him a prodigy, and his grades were excellent. In fact, I hear he was top of his class and captain of the cricket team to boot. And the ladies loved him. His days were rich and full, and he had a bright future ahead of him."

"........."

"Doesn't that sound a bit odd? How could such a promising young man get reduced to a mangy beast like this?"

Purple Ant presented his hand to the bartender, and the bartender gave him a wineglass garnished with a custom-made stun gun. That was Purple Ant's weapon of choice. He flipped it on, and blue sparks crackled at its tip.

"Allow me to demonstrate," he said, then pressed the stun gun against his so-called pet dog's shoulder.

A scream split the air, as bloodcurdling as an echo from Hell itself.

Purple Ant held the stun gun down, and a full twenty-three seconds elapsed. Only then, after tormenting the man for what must have felt like an eternity, did Purple Ant stop the current.

Then he gave the man another order. **"Show me some gratitude."**

Tears rolled down his pet's face as the man groaned in pain. "...Thank you, sir."

"——!"

The captive spy gasped. Her brain couldn't quite process the gruesome spectacle she'd just witnessed.

Purple Ant chuckled. "Shocking, isn't it? You know, there's a trick to tormenting people so they don't pass out."

Stun guns were designed to be powerful enough to knock someone out in a single second. Being able to deliver more than twenty seconds' worth of torture with one required a great deal of finesse.

"I have this gift, you see. For as long as I can remember, I've known exactly what kind of pain will chisel fear deep into a person's brain. Give me a week with someone, and I can make anyone fall in line. If I ordered them to die, they would do just that."

"........."

"He used to be a happy med student, but now, he's just my dog. He gave up his family, his girlfriend, his dreams, and his identity, and now he runs around the world doing exactly what I tell him to."

Purple Ant called that power of his "domination."

The way he saw it, it was a gift he'd been given by God himself.

"The pain I give people rewrites their very brains. It isn't logic that makes them obey me; it's their primal instincts. Students, killers, fighters, bank clerks, and actresses alike all bow before their king," Purple Ant declared. "They become Worker Ants, dutifully obeying me until the day they die."

"........."

"By day, they go about their normal lives. But at night, they serve me like the fanatical slaves they are. They study assassination techniques like their lives depend on it, and they kill without a single scruple or qualm."

Mitario was Purple Ant's stronghold, and he had countless Worker Ants roaming its streets. And what's more, his loyal, unfeeling minions were indistinguishable from normal civilians.

"What I'm saying is, my Worker Ants have already obliterated your team."

With that, Purple Ant began spinning his tale.

He told his captive about the massacre he'd carried out in his kingdom of Mitario.

Chapter 2

Hostilities

Cars people buildings billboards people people people cars buildings cars people people cars cars cars people people trains buildings people people people people people people billboards cars people people cars cars cars people cars people billboards billboards billboards people people buildings trains cars cars people people cars buildings cars people cars people people—

Thea sighed.

Over time, even the jaw-dropping view from her apartment had become just another mundane part of life.

Two weeks had passed since they'd arrived in Mitario, one of the biggest metropolises in the United States of Mouzaia.

Officially, Thea was working as a contract employee for a company in Din that imported foreign furniture. Her cover story was that she, along with Klaus and Grete, were scouring Mitario for information on top-of-the-line furniture they could bring back home with them.

At the moment, they were staying in a pair of deluxe rented apartments. Each one had two bedrooms, and they were right next to each other on the eighth floor of an apartment complex right in the heart of the city.

Main Street ran directly below them, and the morning's traffic was just as gridlocked as always. Hundreds of cars inched forward in ordered lines as the massive billboards along the road advertised products to the rows of drivers. Even the TV news anchors were talking about the congestion and mentioning how the government recommended for commuters to take the subway.

Thea glanced up at the rows of skyscrapers stretching up into the clouds. The Galgad capital's steeples had been impressive, but Mitario was in a whole different league. If one of the skyscrapers was thirty stories tall, then the next would be forty, and the one after that would be fifty, like their builders had been competing or something. Nowadays, nobody ever held the record for "tallest building in the world" for longer than about two years.

It really drives home what a rural backwater we are...

She sighed again.

In the Din Republic, traffic jams happened once in a blue moon, if that. They didn't have television broadcasts, either. Just plain old radio. And they certainly didn't have a subway system. Their big cities had only just gotten commuter trains, and out in the sticks, it wasn't uncommon to see people still riding in horse-drawn carriages. Plus, you could scour the whole country without finding a single building with a double-digit number of floors.

Thea had seen the rows of mega hotels back when she visited the entertainment district in southern Din, but compared to Mitario, even those were little more than dollhouses.

Then she heard Grete's voice from outside her room. "Thea, breakfast is ready..."

After making sure her outfit and hair were all in order, Thea headed over to the dining room. The mouthwatering smell of toast and sweet jam wafted through the air as Grete placed the plates onto a cart.

"Thank you, it looks delicious. Why the cart, though?" Thea asked.

"Oh, this? I made arrangements with the boss for us to eat breakfast together today. I must confess, I'm a little excited."

Once Grete finished loading up the cart, she began pushing it along. Thea presumed she was planning on taking it to the apartment next door, where Klaus was staying.

It made for a delightful sight, but there was one thing that caught Thea's attention.

"Four portions, hmm."

There were four plates laid out alongside one another. All the bread was nicely toasted, but some of the slices were definitely darker than others—perhaps due to restlessness on the part of the cook.

Thea and Grete headed to the neighboring apartment together and knocked on the door. Shortly thereafter, Klaus opened it up. "Good morning to the both of you. I appreciate you going to the trouble."

After thanking Grete, he looked down at the cart.

"Four portions, huh."

Nothing ever got past him.

Grete shook her head in discontent. "...I can't say it brought me much joy."

"You really don't have to go out of your way like this. Starting tomorrow, I'll do the cooking."

The two of them sounded like a pair of heartwarming newlyweds. Thea could watch them for days.

Then an unpleasant voice cut in from the bedroom.

"Ooh, something smells nice. What's that, breakfast? Lucky us, Bonfire! I'm telling you, I'm so hungry I could eat a horse."

Klaus frowned and threw open the bedroom door. "And who said you were getting any?"

Inside, there was a skinny man bound from head to toe—Roland, aka Corpse.

His arms had been placed behind his back, and he was tied up all over in belts held together by an array of locks. Even just the state he was in was already akin to torture, but the elite assassin seemed unperturbed.

He gave them a carefree grin from atop the bed. "Yeesh, man, have a heart. I'm a legitimate informant, remember?"

"Who refuses to give us a lick of actionable intel."

Roland casually brushed off Klaus's snide dig. "Look, just forget about all that and untie me already. I need my hands free to eat toast, you know."

"........." Klaus took the plate of toast and placed in on the ground in front of Roland. "You've got a mouth, haven't you?"

"...Have you ever heard the phrase *POW abuse?*"

"You seriously think captured spies have rights?" Klaus spat as he walked away. He didn't even want to breathe the same room's air as Roland.

"Teach," Thea said, "are you really sure that bringing him was a good idea?"

"He's the only person who knows what Purple Ant looks like. Unfortunately, that makes him valuable to us."

Klaus sounded none too pleased about the fact, and Thea understood full well how he felt. Her opinion of Roland was just as low as his. After all, the man had spent his days killing politicians and covert agents the world over. Who knew just how many people had died at his hands?

All of a sudden, Grete approached Roland holding a knife and a fork. With a stony expression, she began slicing his toast.

Now there was a surprise. Nobody had expected her to actively choose to go wait on him.

Roland thanked her, but Grete ignored him. "I...have a few questions for you."

Her voice was stiff. She had a thing about talking to men.

"Oh yeah?"

"Do you remember Olivia?"

Thea recognized that name. It was the spy Grete had fought. Olivia was Roland's apprentice, and she'd used her position as a major politician's maid to provide support for Imperial spies.

"What? Of course I do," Roland replied. "What about her?"

"Did you...actually love her?"

"Oh yeah, for sure. All I had to do was tell her I loved her, and she was willing to go out and risk her life for me. As far as pawns go, it doesn't get much better than—"

The toast smashed into Roland's face.

And the plate, too, for good measure.

The red strawberry jam looked almost like blood as it trickled down his body.

"Grete," Klaus called over to her. "Calm down."

"Yes, sir... I'm sorry..."

After throwing the plate, Grete left the bedroom and locked it up tight behind her. "Thea, would you be able to look into his heart?" she quietly asked. "The sooner we get that information out of him, the sooner we can dump him into the sea."

"I never realized you were the vengeful type!"

Clearly, Roland had incurred her wrath.

Thea sighed. Grete was usually the one having to calm her down, not the other way around. "I understand how you feel, but I can't. I've tried over and over, but he never lets his guard down."

Thea had a special talent—the ability to peek into the heart of anyone she locked eyes with.

Against elite spies, though, that was easier said than done. She had made countless attempts to use it on Roland, but each one had ended in failure. Every time, he averted his gaze before she could get what she needed out of him. That was probably his spy instincts at work telling him to be careful around her.

"Let's not worry about him for now," Klaus said. "We can find Purple Ant through other means. We know he's meddling with the Tolfa Economic Conference, so starting tomorrow, I'll begin digging into the attendees. Once we find out who Purple Ant is, we'll be able to capture him."

He went on.

"You two are in charge of the others."

Thea and Grete gave him a pair of resolute nods.

"You got it."

"Of course..."

From there on out, it was going to be up to them to determine the team's course of action.

Once she was finished eating, Thea headed back to her and Grete's apartment.

It was eight AM, and now the city was really alive. The sound of car horns echoed up incessantly from the main road. It was the perfect time for spies like them to get to work.

For the past two weeks, they'd devoted themselves to blending in. Thea had worked diligently as a genuine furniture company employee, and she'd actually gone and visited a number of furniture stores. If anyone looked at her, all they would see was a young career woman, and if the police stopped her for questioning, she would have answers for anything they threw at her.

Everything was proceeding right on schedule, and now it was time for the intelligence work to begin.

Thea made some tea and sat down at the dining table. "All right, well, um... Grete, would you mind summing up where we stand at the moment?"

"Of course. I'll get right on it."

With that, Grete took out a notepad and wrote down all the information they currently had.

Mission Name: Mitario Manhunt.

Objective: Capture Purple Ant and gather intel on Serpent.

Assumption: Serpent is getting in touch with important players at the Tolfa Economic Conference and manipulating them for the Empire's benefit.

Agenda 1: Deploy Lamplight members around various important players and have them search for enemy spies.

Agenda 2: Once we find enemy spies, interrogate them to find out where Purple Ant is.

Addendum: Klaus will be acting independently. The plan is for him to do thorough checks on anyone suspicious he runs into.

"Thank you," Thea said. "That does about sum it up, doesn't it?"

After using the note to refresh her memory, she tore out the page and used a match to light it on fire.

Now she had a better handle on what they needed to do—and on just how hard it would be to do it.

"I suppose this goes without saying, but we have an acute shortage of real intel on our opponent. We're basically in the dark here," she noted.

"That is true," Grete replied. "However, we do know where it is we need to be—the Tolfa Economic Conference. The more we dig into it, the more likely we are to run into other spies."

"I wonder what all the operatives from other nations are doing?"

"I suspect we don't need to worry about them. The boss has already gotten in touch with our allied nations. The United States and everyone else on our side already know they need to watch out for the Empire."

Thea nodded.

For the time being, all they needed to focus on was Galgad. If they tried to take on the Lylat Kingdom, the Fend Commonwealth, the United States of Mouzaia, the Bumal Kingdom, and every other attending nation into account, they'd never get anywhere.

"Okay, so the first thing we should check is, um…"

She couldn't get out the words.

She had gone over the whole mission backward and forward, but now her thoughts refused to come together. Her teammates were scattered across the city, and she had no idea what orders to give them.

Am I really fit to command?

There were hundreds of key players at the conference, and if you counted all the other attendees as well, that number swelled to well over ten thousand. Now, it was Thea's job to figure out which ones to tell her allies to investigate. Furthermore, each of Lamplight's members had their own strengths and weaknesses. And what's more, their various infiltration points had different tasks they were suitable for. Thea had to take all of that into account.

There's too much to keep track of!

She clutched at her head.

She couldn't do it. It wasn't possible.

Grete offered her a lifeboat. "…To start off, why don't we check in on everyone?"

"R-right, of course. Let's do that."

"We should probably make sure they carried out their infiltrations successfully before we start giving them orders, I would think."

She made a valid point.

In fact, that was Command and Control 101. Thea was humiliated that she'd let something so basic slip her mind.

"Th-that's our Grete, always on top of things. You know, I was just about to say the same—"

"Of course. Now, these here are their schedules for the day."

Grete handed her a memo pad she'd prepared in advance. On it, there was a complete list of where their teammates would be that accounted for everything from the bus and subway timetables to how gridlocked the roads would be.

That was Grete for you—always diligent and observant.

Actually, that reminded Thea of something.

"Say, Grete. During your last mission, weren't you the one in charge of giving orders?"

"It was just for the one operation, but yes."

Grete, along with Lily, Sybilla, and Sara, had successfully captured an enemy spy alive. And thanks to the detailed instructions she'd given, they had done so without needing to rely on Klaus at all.

To be honest, I wish she could just take over...!

Grete's skills clearly outstripped hers. Thea had left capturing Roland entirely to Klaus, she'd gotten bailed out by Monika during their battle against the Military Intelligence Department, and ultimately, an enemy spy had laughed right in her face.

"Don't worry, Thea. I'm sure you'll do a splendid job."

Despite Grete's encouragement, Thea couldn't muster up a single drop of confidence.

For now, I should just follow Grete's lead...

It was a pathetic cop-out for a commander to take, but Thea didn't know what else to do.

Thea and Grete had lied and said that they were both twenty-three. In truth, they were only eighteen, but being treated as minors would restrict their options in a number of ways. When they headed out onto the Mitario streets, they did so dressed in tailored suits and wearing makeup that made them look older.

The main economic conference wasn't the only thing the city had going on. It was accompanied by a wide array of business-to-business discussions, political fundraising parties, and meetings behind closed doors on issues of military import. All in all, there were probably more than a thousand gatherings of various sizes being held. That was one of the reasons the conference took place over such an extended time frame.

And it wasn't all politics and economics, either. Mitario was also a major cultural hub, and it was home to everything from world-renowned fashion shows to internationally acclaimed film festivals.

All that was to say, there was a huge number of people there. You could hardly so much as walk down the street without bumping into someone or having them bump into you.

The skyscrapers towered over Thea and Grete as they walked past the long lines of gridlocked cars.

Then they spotted a crowd gathering in front of one of the buildings.

It was shocking to see that the city could get even more clamorous than it already was.

It appeared that some foreign nation's minister of foreign affairs had just arrived, and his car had gotten swarmed by paparazzi on its way down to the underground parking lot. Camera flashes lit up the air.

Reporters stood in the car's way and held out mics and voice recorders.

"Minister, what are your thoughts going into this meeting with the Lylat Kingdom?" "I have some questions about the Galgad appeasement policies!"

The old man sitting in the car's back seat responded to their questions with silence and a scowl.

I guess no matter what country you're from, reporters are just as relentless.

Thea's parents ran a newspaper, so it was a sight she was well familiar with. Even so—

"Hey, geezer, we're talkin' to you here! Fuckin' say something already!"

—one young, foul-mouthed reporter in particular caught her attention.

Thea looked at her in shock.

It was Sybilla, dressed in a suit and pounding on the car's window.

Even the minister was taken aback by her attitude. He rolled down the car's window a bit and shouted angrily at her. "Wh-why, I never! What country did you say you're from, girl?!"

"I'm from the Din Republic's *Random Times*, so what? More importantly, do your comments from this morning contradict the department meeting minutes that got published yesterday or what?"

"Excuse me?! Wh-what nonsense are you on about?!"

"Look, I'm just askin' for you to clear up a few—Wait, hey! Quit closin' the window on me! Ow, dammit!"

She thrust her arm through the opened window with a force one would normally expect to see in a fistfight and pointed her mic at his face.

Grete lowered her voice and explained the situation to Thea. "Sybilla is working as a journalist-in-training. Due to her position, she's able to come in contact with politicians and bureaucrats from around the world."

"I see. Well, I just hope she doesn't get herself arrested..."

Thea had some concerns, but it looked like Sybilla had things under control.

The car broke free from the reporters and made its way down into the parking lot. The reporters who'd been surrounding it sighed, then dispersed.

Sybilla was no different. "Damn, he got away," she groaned as she walked toward Thea and Grete.

The moment she passed them by, she slipped something into Thea's pocket. Thea heard a quiet whisper at her ear. "I lifted that minister's card case off him. Hope it's useful."

She must have done it during that brief moment she stuck her arm in the window. Nobody had been any the wiser.

Then, with a nonchalant "all right, where's that next scoop at?" she vanished into the crowd.

By the look of it, Sybilla the reporter was in position to get some good results.

The next place Grete led her to was a restaurant attached to a station.

Inside, Thea could hear a jaunty tune playing. She assumed they had a record on but soon discovered that the music was actually live. There was a jazz band playing atop the stage in the back so the restaurant's patrons could enjoy some live music while they had their lunch.

Mitario was known as the home of jazz, and performances like this weren't uncommon in its restaurants and bars.

For Thea, though, it was her first time hearing jazz music live. It all felt very refined.

The mellow piano tune melded together with the trumpet and the sax, and they all coalesced into a single beautiful harmony. Even though it was a new experience for her, the sound had a very comforting quality to it.

Thea and Grete made their way to a pair of seats right beside the stage.

Now they could see the jazz-playing sextet up close and personal. They were wearing white tailcoats and stylish hats, and the trumpet and piano players looked mighty slick indeed. The rest of the audience clearly shared that impression. In particular, many of the young women present were watching the band members with passion in their eyes.

And the rightmost member of the band...was Monika.

"........."

She was dressed in a man's tailcoat and playing the tenor sax.

She didn't look a bit out of place.

"Apparently, she started out by busking, and she got recruited by the band that very same day," Grete explained.

By that point, Thea was past being surprised. It was Monika they were talking about.

"That band often gets hired to play at parties and social get-togethers thrown by politicians," Grete went on. "From what I hear, they're a huge hit among those politicians' wives..."

In other words, the plan was to have Monika use her position as a musician to carry out her covert activities.

When the band finished the song they were on, Monika stepped down from the stage and walked over to their seats.

"Hey, you two. What's with all the staring? You fans of mine or something?"

"No. Get back onstage already," Thea replied.

"Sorry, girls, but I'm all booked up tonight. Some bigwig hired us to do a concert at this party he's throwing."

She threw them a wink, then returned to the stage. The way she was carrying herself was a bit pompous, but apparently, that was what the ladies liked.

Right before she headed back up, she left a matchbox on the table. There was probably a report written inside.

There could be little doubt that Monika the saxophonist would be an asset they could count on.

After polishing off a light appetizer, the two of them left the restaurant.

Apparently, the plan was to have a proper lunch somewhere else, and Thea had a pretty good idea of where they might be heading. There was one infiltration point where the agent stationed there had loudly requested that particular placement well ahead of time.

Their destination was in the Westport Building, the site of the Tolfa Economic Conference. On its ground floor, it had a large chain hamburger joint that offered outside seating.

Ten minutes after they placed their order, a busty waitress cheerfully brought it over.

"Thank you for waiting! Here are your cheeseburger combo meals."

It was Lily.

She delivered their food dressed in the burger joint's uniform. The burgers were fat and juicy, the fries were mountainous, and the cups of cola were all but overflowing. Lily looked as pleased as punch. For some reason, she seemed to feel right at home surrounded by junk food. Even the trim red-and-white-striped uniform looked good on her.

Grete called over to her. "Excuse me, waitress?"

"Hmm? Did you have a question for me? That is to say, a question for Lillian Hepburn, the eighteen-year-old exchange student who goes to the Mitario University School of Pharmacy, lives alone, and is paying her way with this part-time job?"

Grete was so flabbergasted that she dropped the act. "…I was going to explain who you were, but I suppose you've just saved me the trouble."

However, there was really no need to explain at all. Thea had already known Lily's infiltration point. Lily had been going on for ages about how she wanted to be stationed: "somewhere I can eat all the burgers I want!"

Then someone shouted over from inside the shop. "Hey, Lillian! I need you to bring this up to conference room thirteen on the fourth floor."

"Well, they call it Mitario's favorite food for a reason. The orders just don't stop coming!" Lily said gleefully as she left Thea and Grete to their meal.

That particular branch offered delivery, and with the Westport Building right above them, it was no surprise that they got a lot of orders from the conference attendees.

"Well, it's a relief to see that her infiltration is going well," Thea remarked.

"It is, but...there is one thing I'm slightly concerned about," Grete replied.

"Really? Oh, that reminds me. When you called her over just now, what was that about?"

Grete looked down at the meal Lily had brought her. "This is a fish burger, not a cheeseburger..."

".........."

"I'm a little worried she's going to get herself fired..."

They looked over and saw Lily with a big backpack slung over her shoulder. She was just about to go on her delivery run. "Lillian, over and out!" she shouted as she ran off.

She was supposed to be bringing the food to conference room thirteen on the fourth floor.

However, the elevator Lily triumphantly boarded was heading down to the underground parking lot.

When they got back to their apartment that evening, Thea let out a long sigh.

"Now we have the board in order."

There were a number of points she wanted to quibble about, but all in all, things seemed to be going according to plan. Now it was up to them to dole out orders and track down Purple Ant.

She didn't want to spend much effort on dinner, so she took a can of minestrone and popped it in a pot of water, can and all. As the water boiled, Thea strained her ears to hear what was going on in the apartment next door. She couldn't pick up anything. Klaus must still be out and about.

"We need to spend the evening thinking about how we want to proceed going forward," Thea remarked. "I'd love to be able to bounce ideas off Teach, but I doubt he'll be back anytime soon."

"I just hope he isn't overworking himself..."

Grete sliced up a baguette and popped the pieces in the oven. Her voice quivered with concern.

Thea gave her a smile. "If he is, then it'll give you a chance to soothe his fatigue. Once we're done here, I'll teach you a massage that men just die for. This time, he'll be like putty in your hands for sure."

The moment the subject turned to romance, Grete's expression immediately brightened.

"Oh, Thea... Thea the Brilliant and Wise, I can't thank you enough."

"The key is to focus on the groin area."

"Come to think of it, Monika warned me that I should stop taking your advice."

"Oh yeah? And what does she know?"

"Oh, wise one. You always know just what to say!"

Taking part in their usual back-and-forth helped calm Thea's nerves. There was only so long she could spend with her nose to the grindstone before it started wearing her out.

Then they heard something smack into their window.

Grete seemed to have some idea of what it was. She rushed happily over to the windowsill.

"What is it, Grete?"

"The boss brought us some intel."

There was a rock lying outside their window with a newspaper wrapped around it. It was the same paper you could buy on any old street corner, but it had a secret cipher written on it in special ink. The question was, how had he gotten it all the way up to the eighth floor? Had he seriously thrown it?

Grete read through the message. Her breath got caught in her throat. "...We might find ourselves face-to-face with the enemy a lot sooner than we expected."

"What does it say?"

"Our allied nations' agents are getting taken out one after another. Apparently, there are a number of skilled spy hunters lurking in the city."

Thea quickly skimmed over the encoded text.

According to the message, tons of people were getting murdered, dying under suspicious circumstances, and going missing. And what's more, the vast majority of the victims were intelligence agents who'd been investigating the Tolfa Economic Conference.

Furthermore, the murder methods were all over the spectrum. There was everything from stabbings and fatal falls to suicides, disappearances, and even traffic accidents. There was no discernible pattern to it.

It wasn't clear if Purple Ant was the one behind it all, but there could be no doubt that someone was going around killing people.

Thea was worried about their teammates' safety.

"Wh-what should we do?"

"We'll have to keep closely in touch with the others," Grete said calmly. "That way, we'll be able to use my disguises and your negotiation skills to rush to their aid if anything happens. And if worse comes to worst, we might have no choice but to get help from the boss."

"M-makes sense. I'll make sure to be ready to act at a moment's notice."

"Even so, there's only so much we'll be able to do for them… In a lot of cases, we'll have to just trust them to handle things on their own."

Thea felt her gaze drift toward the window as though drawn there by Grete's words. "True enough…"

Night had fallen on Mitario, and neon lights filled the city. The main road's bright billboards ensured that the city never slept.

As they spoke, their teammates were doubtless still hard at work.

Then, two weeks after the mission began in earnest…all of Thea's worries came true.

It started in the hotel across from the Westport Building.

It was an upscale hotel favored by many of the conference's attendees, and it had a bar on its second floor where you could order spirits and light meals. Not only did all its seating come in the form of private rooms, but the rooms were also soundproofed, making them perfect for patrons who wanted to share meals or have conversations without being overheard. Its clientele ranged from politicians and bureaucrats to captains of industry.

Each of the rooms was outfitted with leather sofas, a glass table, and a gorgeous overhead light fixture.

Sybilla sank her teeth into her plate of spareribs, enthusiastically munching down on the heavily seasoned salty-sweet meat and leaving behind nothing but well-cleaned bones.

She wiped her hands. "You're really sure you don't mind treating me to all this?" she asked with a smile.

There was a stocky older man sitting across from her. "Oh, no, not at all. With the way you saved my bacon, this is the least I can do. Please, don't hold back! Here, try something from this menu next."

"For real? You're a lifesaver, man. In that case, I'll go for this one here, third from the top on the left."

"Ah, the perfect choice for a youngster like you. I love it!" The man laughed heartily and quaffed down the rest of his wine.

He was a vice president at a Bumal Kingdom tea manufacturer, and he had come to the conference alongside a Bumal Kingdom diplomat to help negotiate the tariff rate on luxury goods being exported out of Tolfa. While he was there, he had also been in discussions with a few other countries about opening food processing plants within their borders.

He was a talented man in many regards but sloppy in others—such as how he'd left all his classified documents in an easily stolen briefcase.

"I must say, that almost ended quite badly for me. I never imagined someone would steal my briefcase right out of that coffee shop. If you hadn't gallantly come along and retrieved it, I don't know what might have become of me!"

"Nah, it was nothin'. Heck, I wasn't even able to catch the guy who did it."

"Details, details. This is about me wanting to show you my gratitude."

"In that case, what would you say to givin' me an exclusive one-on-one?"

"I wouldn't mind one bit. If you have questions, then ask away, ask away."

"That's mighty generous of ya. With a heart like that, you'll be president in no time."

"Oh, you can skip the flattery. I'm still just a humble VP."

Continuing to play the part of the newspaper columnist, Sybilla began asking the man interview questions. The VP was clearly a chatty man, and he told her all sorts of things she hadn't even asked about. Every nod and "mm-hmm" Sybilla gave him seemed to brighten his mood more, and he guzzled down booze at an ever-increasing pace.

On his urging, Sybilla had a beer as well.

By the time half an hour had passed, the VP was well and truly plastered. "Gotta shay, I'm real exshited about this interview. You *are* going to publish it, right?"

Sybilla gave his slurred question a confused laugh. "Of course. I'm goin' to all the trouble of writing it, aren't I?"

"Will you really, though? I've done one-on-ones with a whooole buncha journalists, and they never went to print."

"...Oh yeah?"

"I dunno *why* for the life of me. I guess I'm just unlucky, but nunna the journalishts even return my calls. 'S just plain rude's what it is."

".........."

Sybilla scratched her forehead a bit. The sharp stimulus helped her focus her senses.

"Hey, not to change the subject—"

She gestured with her pen.

"—but who's that behind you?"

Sybilla and the VP weren't the only ones in the room.

There was also the VP's secretary, as well as a man standing wordlessly behind him.

The man's skin was as tight as a drum, and even through his clothes, it was easy to picture how incredibly toned his muscles were. His button-down shirt was at its limits just trying to contain his bulging biceps.

"Hmm? Oh, him. That's Barron, my chauffeur."

Barron nodded a little. "*Oui.* Don't mind me."

Sybilla gave him a small wave. "His voice is kinda gloomy, but his pronunciation's really good. Is he local?"

"That's right. My usual chauffeur was s'pposed to come over from home, too, but he got a bad case of food poisoning. Had to find a replacement in a hurry. Barron here might look scary, but he's good at what he does, both behind the wheel and away from it."

"...*Oui.*"

The VP popped a cigarette in his mouth to demonstrate, and Barron immediately offered him a lighter. Apparently, driving wasn't the only thing he took care of for his client.

"........."

"Ah, you worried 'cause he's sho big? Up 'til a few years ago, he was a middleweight boxer. I hear he was *quite* accomplished."

"*Oui.* But I tore a ligament and had to retire."

"What a shame. Ooh, you think you could write an article about that? Or is it a little too inside basheball?"

Sybilla and Barron ignored the VP's drunken rambling and exchanged a glance.

Then their waiter arrived with a fresh bottle of wine.

Barron was already closest to the door, so he took the bottle. "*Oui.* I will pour."

The interview came to an end when Sybilla started feeling queasy.

"Ugh, I don't feel so good..."

"That one might be on me. Sorry for makin' ya drink sho much," the VP said apologetically as Sybilla covered her mouth with her hand. "Barron, give the nice reporter a ride back to her plashe, will you?"

Sybilla quickly waved him off. "No, no, you really don't need to."

"It's fine, it'sh fine. Perfect excuse to keep the party goin'. Now, make sure you give me a call once you've got a date set for that article, you hear?"

The VP strolled away merrily with his secretary in tow. They were heading off in search of female companionship, no doubt.

That left Sybilla and Barron alone in front of the hotel bar.

"*Oui.* This way."

"Thanks."

According to Barron, the car was parked beneath the hotel.

Sybilla followed his directions and tottered unsteadily on the dark stairs. On the way down, she lost her footing, bumping into Barron a few times. He didn't seem pleased about it, but he helped support her all the same.

Once they were all the way underground, Sybilla rushed over to a gutter. "Urgh, I can't take it anymore."

She vomited out the contents of her stomach. Everything she'd eaten and drunk back in the room came out the same way it had gone in.

Beside her, Barron frowned. "...*Oui*. I'll get you some water."

He headed back to the stairs. On his way up, he fished for something in his breast pocket, then let out a quiet sound of confusion. Whatever he'd been searching for, it wasn't there.

"Lookin' for this?" Sybilla called out to him.

There were a couple of small pills resting on her fingertip.

"Sleeping pills, huh? That's some messed-up stuff you were slippin' me."

"........."

"I had to throw up in a hurry, or that coulda gone bad. All right, who put you up to this? I can't imagine it was that VP."

Sybilla was already certain of Barron's guilt.

Back when the VP had brought up the journalists who'd gone missing, Barron's expression had shifted ever so slightly. He knew something. And on top of that, there were the drugs he'd slipped into the wine. When he poured it, he had made sure to position the bottle in a way that hid his hand.

He was no ordinary chauffeur.

"Now, tell me who your client is, or I'll call the police and tell 'em what you—"

Sybilla was cut off mid-sentence.

Barron had just turned tail and dashed up the stairs.

Sybilla had no intention of letting him get away without a fight. She clicked her tongue, then ran after him. Her drunkenness and poor physical form had all been an act. Now it was time to use those leg muscles she'd trained so tirelessly.

However, Barron was no slowpoke, either.

Upon reaching the ground floor, he shoved a few hotel employees aside and fled out the back exit.

Looks like that story about tearing his ligament was all bullshit. Just who the hell is this guy?

Sybilla had more questions than ever as she charged through the back exit in hot pursuit.

Behind the hotel, there was a worn-down, eight-story, multi-tenant building. Barron dashed up its exterior staircase, and Sybilla drew her gun and continued following him. Once she backed him into a corner, she'd be able to pump him for information.

Her foe seemed to have entered the building on its sixth floor. The door was unlocked.

"You're not goin' anywhere!" Sybilla shouted as she charged inside.

Inside, there was an office complex that looked like it was scheduled for demolition. There were no tenants inside, and all the offices were vacant. That said, it still had power, and there were fluorescent lights illuminating its hallways.

A long corridor stretched out in front of her. Sybilla didn't see anyone there.

Why can't I hear his footsteps anymore? Hell, I can't hear anything... *Is he hiding somewhere?*

She assumed his plan was to launch a surprise attack, so she clasped her gun tight as she strode down the corridor.

All of a sudden, she heard something collapsing out on the exterior staircase.

The next moment, the lights went out.

"Huh?"

The moment after she yelped, something large shifted behind her. She leaped to the side on pure reflex to dodge it, and she felt something whiz by her face.

"*Oui,*" Barron said calmly.

Sybilla whirled around and tried to put some distance between them. However, she only made it a few steps before stumbling over something. The visibility was terrible. After tumbling onto the floor, she fled into one of the unoccupied offices.

Dammit, for real? Well, at least I know what's goin' on...

She realized now that he had lured her there on purpose, but it was too late. She was already in his hunting grounds.

It was pitch-black there.

All of the building's windows were boarded up. Not even a single ray of light from outside could make it in, and she couldn't see a thing. Her eyes were useless. All she had to rely on were the tiniest of sounds to find the hulking mass of murder approaching her.

"I've trained long and hard to be able to fight without needing to see," Barron muttered.

After that, everything went silent for a bit. Then a mighty fist bore down on her from behind.

It took everything Sybilla had just to sense the attack a moment before it landed so she could avoid suffering a direct hit. Even still, the force from the blow was so fierce, she felt like her whole body was going to get blown away.

"This prison of darkness will be your grave."

As Barron's voice echoed out, she sensed the next invisible blow coming. But she had no way to dodge it.

Shit... I seriously can't see a—

It was there in that lightless darkness that Sybilla realized she was going to die.

Meanwhile, over in the Lylat embassy...

The embassy sat in the nicest part of the city, and there was a party being held there to celebrate the anniversary of the Lylat Kingdom's founding. The Lylat conference attendees were far from home, but they threw a big shindig nonetheless and invited all sorts of foreign dignitaries so they could deepen their ties.

In addition to the other guests, Monika's jazz band had been invited to the party. A bureaucrat they were on friendly terms with had insisted that they come help liven things up. His request for them to play jazz versions of a bunch of Lylat classics had been an unusual one, but they rose to the occasion and still delivered a performance for the ages.

After they finished playing, the band stuck around and made pleasant conversation with the partygoers. Several of the attendees had brought their families along, and the jazz players took it upon themselves to entertain the children by dancing around and playing music with them. According to Monika's fellow band members, going the extra mile like that was the trick to landing repeat gigs.

Monika chose to do likewise. She mingled with the crowd, showing off her tenor sax skills while freely giving out the bright smiles she was normally so stingy with. "If you like what you hear, feel free to hire us for your next parties!" she suggested to the various nations' officials she crossed paths with.

As she was making connections, someone spoke to her from behind.

"That performance you gave was really something. I gotta say, it really pulled me in."

The speaker was a young woman who looked to be just north of a decade older than Monika. She had long, flowing blond hair and was wearing a dress that left her shoulders almost bare.

"Thanks," Monika replied cordially. "You were, uh…"

"Miranda. I'm just a college student; one of the old guys brought me as his date."

There was a libertine nonchalance to the way she offered Monika her hand.

As Monika returned her handshake, Miranda leaned in and whispered conspiratorially. "So, you trying to hook up with the fat cats here? Maybe do a little gold digging?"

"Nah, that's not my scene." Monika shook her head. "The band's still trying to make a name for itself. Gotta pound the pavement to get those gigs, you know?"

"Really? I heard you guys were pretty famous already."

"Oh yeah? To tell you the truth, I only just joined up," Monika replied, sticking her tongue out bashfully.

Miranda gave her a toothy laugh. "Girl, I like your style. I think you and I could get along just fine."

"Well, hey, that makes two of us."

"Say, you want to get out of here?" Miranda whispered in her ear. "I've got somewhere nice I want to show you. You'll love it—lots of folks with deep pockets."

Monika licked her lips. "Tell me more."

The two of them slipped out of the party, and Miranda led her to an alleyway just outside of Mitario's business district. After they passed by a series of cramped-looking bars and bordellos, they reached a coffee shop.

Miranda flashed the manager a coin, and he let them through into the back. From there, they headed down a staircase leading underground and arrived at a large door.

It swung open and revealed the large hall within.

It was well lit inside, and there were nearly fifty people there with their faces flushed red and their voices raised.

They were crowded around a series of tables featuring cards, roulette, dice games, and slot machines. Every so often, someone would cheer with joy, and a scantily clad woman would slide them a big pile of chips.

"An underground casino, huh?" Monika lit up. "I love it. Feels like the kind of place where people would let all sorts of secrets slip."

Over at the poker table, the Fend Commonwealth vice minister of foreign affairs was sitting next to the president of a Mouzaian pharmaceutical company, and they were far from the only conference attendees in the room.

Miranda smiled proudly. "You want me to put in a good word for you? I'm friends with the owner, and I bet I could get 'im to let your band play here."

"You'd really do that? Man, where have you been all my life?"

Miranda handed her something. "Here, take these."

That something turned out to be three small arrows about as long as her hand.

"Huh? Darts?"

"Yeah. It'll grease the wheels better if you play a round before I introduce you. Have you ever played before?"

"Heh. Wouldn't you like to know?" Monika replied, dodging the question as she followed after Miranda.

There was a pair of dartboards hung up in the corner of the hall surrounded by men who looked to be the casino's bookies. They were all wearing masks that covered the right halves of their faces.

"The game's dead simple. You just throw the darts at the target." Miranda stood in front of one of the dartboards and positioned herself perpendicular to it. "Like so."

Moving only her elbow, she threw her three darts one after another.

Monika had a decent grasp on the rules. All of Miranda's darts sank into the triple 20, the highest-scoring spot on the board—which was only a half-inch square.

There was a large blackboard hanging next to the dartboard, and Miranda's feat earned her a 180 on hers.

Monika followed Miranda's lead and stood in front of the dartboard beside hers. She thought she saw the bookie smirking, but she ignored him and readied her darts. Then she positioned herself the same way Miranda had and threw them using only the power of her elbow.

"Like this?"

One after another, Monika's shots landed in the triple 20.

Miranda's expression stiffened. "...W-wow. You're pretty good at this."

A masked man retrieved her darts, then wrote a 180 on her blackboard just like Miranda's.

From there, Miranda and Monika continued taking turns throwing sets of three darts. Neither of them ever missed the triple 20, and in no time at all, each blackboard was covered in a long series of 180s.

Before long, a crowd started gathering and letting out cries of amazement at Monika's and Miranda's incredible techniques.

"Who are these ladies?"

"I can't believe it..."

"How do they keep hitting that tiny spot?"

"What's wrong with these chicks?"

"So, how do we know who wins?" Monika asked once she finished her seventh round. By that point, she had successfully hit twenty-one triple 20s in a row.

Miranda, who had matched her score every step of the way, readied her darts again. "Normally it ends after eight rounds, and the winner is whoever has the higher score."

"What if it's a tie?"

"We go into overtime."

"Wait, this game sucks. We'll have to keep playing for the rest of our lives," Monika replied in exasperation before throwing her darts again.

Sure enough, the match quickly stretched into overtime. The blackboards got wiped clean, only to be populated with a fresh round of 180s.

After the ninth and tenth rounds ended the exact same way, Miranda loudly clicked her tongue. "Just as a warning, I'd be careful about scoring too many more points."

Monika frowned. "Oh yeah? Why's that?"

"Down here, we play for keeps. The loser has to pay up to the tune of a hundred donnies for every point the winner gets."

Monika took another look over at the blackboards.

After ten rounds, she had a total score of 1,800. If you multiplied that by a hundred of Mouzaia's donny currency, it came out to a sum roughly four times what an average adult man made in a year.

Yeah, I figured that was what was going on.

However, the expression she put on was one of heartbroken betrayal. Her lips twitched. "What the hell, Miranda? I didn't agree to any bet."

"You agreed to it the moment you walked in that door." Miranda triumphantly threw her darts. Her score for the tenth round was, yet again, 180. "If you don't have the cash, you can always pay with your body. This place does strip shows, too."

"I didn't agree to that, either."

"They're pretty gnarly, though. They've got this big old guillotine they like to use to dissect the performers."

At that point, Monika noticed that there were more masked men around than earlier, and they were positioning themselves to box her in. The bookies probably all belonged to some local gang, and they were clearly no strangers to violence. It was their job to capture the loser.

The onlookers began grinning evilly in anticipation of Monika's defeat.

Losing would mean getting dissected live onstage. There was no guarantee she'd even walk away with her life.

She shrugged and lined up her darts. "I'll never understand the stuff rich people are into."

Miranda watched her with a sadistic smile. "I hate to break it to you, but you're not the first prodigy I've gone up against. It's rare, but it happens."

"........"

"The thing is, though, people are funny creatures. Even if you're a prodigy who can throw a perfect game like it's nothing, the moment you get stuck in a life-and-death situation, you fall apart in no time. Me, though, I'm totally fine. This is exactly what I've trained for."

"........"

"Now, let's see how long you can keep cool now that you know the—"

"So, if you look at it another way..." Monika ignored Miranda's jeers and threw her next dart. It landed smack-dab in the middle of the triple 20. "Then if *I* win, I'll have you at my mercy just like that. That's what I like to hear."

"......!"

"This works out nicely. I gotta say, I was pretty darn curious about why you came after me."

Monika's second and third darts struck home as well.

"The thing is, you picked the wrong mark. Once I take you down, I can just *make* you tell me."

"Sounds like *someone's* getting ahead of themselves."

With that, the two monsters began their battle in earnest.

No matter how many rounds passed, the both of them continued racking up perfect 180-point scores. It got to the point where the dartboards were coming apart from being hit in the same spot so many times and had to be replaced.

Up through the fifteenth round, the spectators continued hooting and hollering in excitement. Around when the twentieth round arrived, though, the voices started dying down. They had started to realize what it was they were watching—a fight to the death between two people who had transcended human limitations.

Now every person in the hall was gathered around them, waiting with bated breath to see how the match would end.

It was the twenty-seventh round where fortune's winds shifted.

That was the round where Monika's third throw ended up veering low.

"What the—?!" she exclaimed.

Her dart had landed in one of the single 20 sections.

It flew wrong...?

She hadn't made any errors in her form, yet she had missed her mark.

Something must have interfered with it in midair. There was no other way to explain it.

"Well, well, well. Sorry, but that's game over."

Miranda gave her a suspicious-sounding laugh, then readied her third dart.

It went without saying that her first and second throws had been perfect. As long as she scored at least twenty-one points with her third throw, she would secure the win.

"Make sure you watch closely. This is the moment where your whole life ends."

As the crowd watched expectantly, she threw the decisive dart.

An hour before Sybilla and Monika had their run-ins with their foes, another event took place in Mitario.

Up on the Westport Building's third floor, Lily got a hunch that she would come face-to-face with an opponent soon.

It happened while she was delivering burgers and doing her espionage work.

"Ah, sorry. I got the wrong room again."

"I feel I see you do that a lot…"

Lily could move freely throughout the building, and all it cost her was some exasperation from the conference big shots. By "accidentally" entering the wrong room, it gave her an opportunity to set up her handiwork.

All right, got the bug in place.

The moment she opened the door, she stuck her device to the bottom of the table. Pretending to be a scatterbrained waitress was a job she was uniquely suited for. Plus, it gave her a ready-made excuse for the times when she really did misremember what room she was supposed to go to.

She apologized and made to leave the room. Before she could, though, someone called over to her. "Hey, kid, hold up."

"Hyeep! Yes?" she replied nervously.

The man snickered. He was a bureaucrat from the United States' Ministry of Economy, Trade, and Industry. "There's no need to get so defensive. I just wanted to pick your brain about this rumor I heard."

"Really?"

"Yeah, I was wondering if you knew anything about this 'hero of Mitario' people are talking about. Supposedly, this hero swoops in to lend a helping hand when people need them most. You ever hear your friends talking about anything like that?"

Lily had never heard anything of the sort. "I haven't, but then, I did just arrive from overseas."

She pressed him for details just in case, but it turned out to be little more than an urban legend. Apparently, little bits and pieces of information were flying around town.

As the story went, there was a hero—someone who only appeared to people who were in the depths of despair. Someone who offered them hope and liberty.

Lily cocked her head. "Someone who offers liberty... So, kinda like the big statue in the harbor?"

The man laughed. "Ha-ha. You might be onto something there."

It was a nice rumor, but Lily found it hard to imagine it being relevant to her mission. She asked him if he knew any more specifics just to be on the safe side, then left the room.

She was getting on the elevator and idly fantasizing about the hero, when all of a sudden—

"Huh?"

—a chill ran down her spine.

It wasn't because of anything she'd seen. Still, she could definitely sense some sort of change in the air.

She licked her dry lips.

I guess after all that training I did, I'm finally developing a spy's intuition.

Thinking about it, Klaus often got through his missions on hunches and *I just did*s.

It would seem that she'd developed a similar sixth sense of her own.

Someone's coming...and they're not friendly!

Lily took a deep breath and braced herself for battle.

She got out of the elevator, but she still didn't see any foes.

However, she was certain that her hunch was accurate. She returned to the burger shop.

"Oh, hey, Lillian, you've got a visitor," one of her coworkers said when she got back. "There's someone who says they want to talk to you."

Lily couldn't think of anyone who would come asking for her like that.

"You can take off early. They're waiting for you out back."

"You got it," Lily replied with a nod. She headed over to her locker in the back of the store.

Well, I definitely didn't expect them to come at me so brazenly...

She opened her backpack's false bottom and retrieved her handgun from within, then stashed it in her leg holster and covered it up with her uniform's skirt.

She clapped her cheeks to brace herself.

It's okay. I got this. I'm gonna take all the skills Teach taught me and turn the tables on 'em!

Losing wasn't an option.

The other girls were probably going up against fierce foes as well, and it was her job as team leader to be the first one to overcome her opponent.

It was go time.

She headed over to the back of the building and found a man and a woman each wearing a suit and an overcoat. Lily didn't recognize them, but she could tell by the keen look in their eyes that these were no ordinary civilians. Their faces had that grizzled look to them exclusive to those who operated in the world of violence.

Lily could feel it in her bones—these two were no pushovers.

She let out a long exhale and traced her fingers over her gun through the skirt. "You two, is it? I gotta give you credit; it was pretty sporting of you to come at me head-on like—"

"Hello, ma'am. We're with the Mitario Police Department."

"Huh?"

That wasn't the line Lily had been expecting them to lead with. She tilted her head in puzzlement.

The police?

True, they did look the part of police detectives. And they were holding up the proper ID, too.

"………"

Lily went silent for a bit as she tried to logic the situation out.

She quickly arrived at her conclusion.

"I see, I see. Pretty bold of you to pose as detectives." She scoffed. "Did you seriously think I wouldn't see through those disguises?"

"Huh?"

"What?"

Something didn't quite fit. The man and the woman looked at her in confusion, and it didn't seem like they were acting.

Only then did Lily put the pieces together.

"W-wait, you're actually real cops?!"

"What are you talking about?" the male detective said, frowning. "Look, I'm going to cut to the chase. You're wanted as a suspect in a murder case. Would you mind coming with us?"

"A suspect in a *what*?!"

"There's an eyewitness who says you shot two people dead the day before yesterday." The female detective fished a document out of her pocket and showed it to Lily. "We have a warrant out for your arrest."

The warrant was the real deal. It was stamped with the official seal of a United States of Mouzaia court, and it authorized the detention of a one Lillian.

The thing was, Lily obviously hadn't committed any murders of the sort.

It was then, at long last, that she realized what was going on. In all likelihood, their enemies were behind this.

"B-but it's not true! This is a conspiracy set up by a Galgad spy!"

She desperately tried to plead her innocence, but the detectives just frowned at her.

"…Is there something wrong with her?"

"We should probably test her for drugs."

"But I'm telling you the truth here!"

"Look, kid, if you're going to lie, at least try to make it believable. Why would an Imperial spy go after some exchange student who works at a burger shop?"

"That's, uh, that's a good question…"

She couldn't exactly come out and tell them she was a spy.

"Um…" She smiled sweetly. "Well, why do you think?"

"We should take her in."

"Yup."

"You're heartless! S-stay away from—"

The detectives crept toward her, and Lily swung her arms about. Then she accidentally hit her thigh.

Clunk.

Her pistol fell out of her leg holster and toppled to the ground.

"«««   »»»»
...................."

All three people present looked down at the gun in silence.

The male detective cleared his throat and glanced at his watch. "Um, Lillian Hepburn?"

"…That's me."

"The time is eight forty-seven PM, and I'm placing you under arrest for suspected murder."

He clicked the handcuffs tightly around her wrists.

Lily had been captured.

Three members of the team—Sybilla, Monika, and Lily—were in three different forms of peril.

"………"

Thea stood by the window and gazed out at the Mitario cityscape.

There was an apprehension eating at her that refused to go away.

Her teammates hadn't sent in their regular reports. The system was that once a day, each of them was supposed to use a specific method to send back the intel they'd gathered. Then Thea and Grete could use that intel to inform their next orders.

Today, though, the scheduled time had come and gone, and there was no intel to be seen.

Something was wrong. Sybilla, Monika, and Lily had run into trouble.

"Are they all right, do you think? What should we do?" she asked Grete, who was looking down at the big map spread out across the dining table.

Grete's expression was just as grave as hers. "That's a good question… We all share a common weakness, so I'm a little bit concerned."

"We do?"

What was she talking about?

She gave Grete an inquisitive look, and Grete nodded. "None of us has had any proper defensive training."

"Ah…"

That made perfect sense.

Their training regimen had revolved around defeating Klaus, so it had placed a huge emphasis on gathering intel on a known enemy and using it to attack them. They hadn't developed the skills and talents required to defend themselves against an unknown foe.

"Because of that," Grete continued, "I fear we might be especially vulnerable when we come under attack."

".........."

Thea was reminded of the Annette Incident.

Back then, she was played for a fool because of her inability to see Annette's mom for who she really was. They succeeded in breaking through the Military Intelligence Department's net, but doing so had led them right into their enemy's trap. It was a painful memory, and Grete was exactly right—they lacked the experience necessary to defend themselves from enemy attacks.

Right now, her teammates might be losing in that exact same way.

Thea started to gnaw on her lip as she feared the worst.

"Don't worry. I'm sure they'll all capture their opponents and bring us back some valuable information." Grete smiled. "We have a countermeasure in place for just such an occasion. After all, a small spy can make a big difference."

Thea thought back. Grete had devised a plan as she strolled around the city.

Grete gave her an elegant nod. "And on top of that, if there's one time where we truly shine—"

Grete's tactic produced an immediate change on all three battlefields.

Over behind the Westport Building, Lily was being wrestled into a patrol car.

"Ughhhhh, this is all a setup. I'm telling you, it's an Imperial scheme!"

"You're still going on about your conspiracy theory?" the female detective replied as Lily began crying in earnest.

"Hey, kid," the male detective said. "What's with that stuffed animal hanging on your back?"

Lily cocked her head. "Huh?"

When she looked back over her shoulder, she discovered that someone had stuck a stuffed cat onto her.

But who?

As Lily pondered the mystery, the stuffed animal suddenly emitted a blast of smoke.

"Yo, Sis, time to book it!" she heard someone exclaim happily from amid the fumes.

The sound of a stun gun crackled through the air, and the two detectives crumpled to the ground.

A moment later, Lily let herself get pulled away, and she and Annette began making their grand escape.

Down in the underground casino, Monika and Miranda were having a darts match.

"Ah!"

Miranda's third shot of the twenty-seventh round skewed a little high.

It ended up scoring the same as Monika's had—a single 20. With that, their scores remained equal, and the overtime rounds continued.

Miranda let out a red-faced shout. "Th-there was a mouse! It just threw itself against my ankle!"

"Really? That's the excuse you're going with?" Monika mocked her as though she'd planned it all.

As she did, she silently complimented her teammate. She knew that somewhere among the thronging spectators, there was a girl squeezing her fists together as tight as she could.

Nice one, Sara. Sneaking all the way down here must've taken a lot of guts.

Monika flashed a surreptitious thumbs-up.

Over in the crowd, Sara clandestinely retrieved her mouse and smiled.

Up in the darkened office building, Sybilla and Barron were squaring off.

By all rights, his punch should have been unavoidable.

Sybilla's training let her operate just fine in low-light environments, but pitch darkness was a whole different story. With no ability to see at all, she had no way to counteract Barron's attack.

She could tell from the sound that the blow would knock her dead.

Unless, that was, someone grabbed her and yanked her backward.

She tumbled to the ground, just barely avoiding the attack. Barron's massive fist passed right in front of her eyes. Afterward, her savior tugged on her arm, and Sybilla followed her and took off at a run.

However, her savior couldn't see in the dark, either. With a loud *wham*, they crashed into a wall.

"How unlucky...," Erna moaned.

"Not from where I'm standing, it wasn't. You did good."

Sybilla patted Erna's head and backed herself up against the wall. If she could just reach a corner, it would limit the number of directions from which her foe could approach.

"*Oui.* Backup, hmm?" Barron's voice boomed from the darkness accompanied by the raw bloodlust of a ruthless killer. "It doesn't change anything. You two will never escape this prison of darkness."

He was right. The situation was still overwhelmingly in his favor.

Sybilla was fighting to the death in the dark against a boxer who could move around freely. It would be no exaggeration to call the situation desperate.

However, she didn't so much as falter. What could she possibly have to fear? She had spent ages fighting a man who was leagues stronger than Barron.

"Tough luck, man, but the moment you failed to take us out with that first hit was the moment you sealed your doom."

A dauntless smile spread across her face as she raised her fists.

By a strange twist of fate, her next line was the exact same as the one Grete had said in another part of the city.

"See, if there's one time where we truly shine—it's when we go on the attack."

Across all three of Mitario's battlefields, the girls were beginning their counteroffensive.

Chapter 3

Hero

Down in the underground casino, there wasn't a patron or employee present who didn't have their eyes glued to the fierce battle between the cerulean-haired Monika and the debauchee college student Miranda.

The twenty-seventh round was over now, and their scores were equal. Everyone had assumed that Monika's failure to hit the triple 20 on her third dart of the round would be how the match ended, but Miranda's last dart had missed the mark as well. Aside from that one throw, though, both of them had continued racking up perfect scores.

Each of their tallies stood at 4,820.

That meant that the loser was already going to be on the hook for 482,000 donnies. There was no way anyone could pay a sum like that. Whoever lost would be facing strip show dismemberment for sure.

The next life-and-death overtime round was about to start, and the audience watched intently.

Meanwhile, Monika fiddled with her forelocks as she tried to come up with a plan.

This isn't looking good...

The problem was what happened in the twenty-seventh round.

For some reason, her third dart had veered low.

It looked like it was some sort of wind. They must have the AC in here rigged...and Miranda must have an accomplice among the bookies. Well, this is a problem. And now, she'll be watching out for Sara's mice.

The next time Monika missed, it really would spell her defeat.

She needed to figure out a way to overcome Miranda's cheating so she could beat her and interrogate her about who she was working for.

Miranda grinned like she had already won. "Come on, aren't you going to throw?"

She had already finished her portion of round twenty-eight. As was to be expected, she had scored a perfect 180.

"Or what, are you too scared? Gosh, I hope your darts don't go flying the wrong way again."

"So it *was* you."

"Who, me? I'm sure I don't have any idea what you're talking about. But let me tell you a secret: Down here, all that matters is where your darts land."

"Eh, maybe I shouldn't have been so worried. I figured out a counter."

If anything, Miranda's taunting had helped clear her head.

Monika held her three darts tight and took her spot in front of her board.

She stared at the target and looked at the dust motes dancing in front of it. She could see how irregular their flight paths were. Sure enough, there was a strong wind blowing in front of her dartboard and hers alone.

Trying to account for the wind's influence was beyond her.

No, the solution Monika had reached was far simpler than that.

A gasp rose up from the audience. "What?"

By all rights, what Monika was doing should have been unthinkable. She lifted both her arms high in the air. Next, she bent her left knee and raised it until it was level with her hips. From there, she leaned her whole body back, then snapped forward.

As the crowd stared at her in disbelief, Monika swung her arm forward and hurled the dart with all her might.

A loud *thunk* rang out. The dart had struck true.

Monika smiled. "Oh, nice, it worked."

The spectators had seen a lot of incredible things that day, but none had been more astonishing than the miracle they'd just witnessed.

It had reminded them all of one thing—Mouzaia's national sport.

"D-did you seriously just...?" Miranda stammered.

"I saw it on one of those TV relay broadcasts last night. It's called the 'windup position,' right?"

The stance she'd chosen was that of a baseball pitcher. By using an overhand throw and putting the strength of her entire body behind it, she had launched the dart like a fastball and cleaved straight through the wind. With speed like that, no obstruction could stand in her way. Her second and third darts made sounds just as satisfying as they sank into the triple 20.

"____!"

Miranda was at a loss for words. And the audience was, too. Monika's stance went against everything they knew about darts theory. Maintaining precise aim with throws like that shouldn't have been possible.

"That was just a fluke! You'll never be able to keep that up!" Miranda cried.

"Won't I?"

Sure enough, Monika did just that.

The twenty-ninth, thirtieth, thirty-first, and thirty-second rounds went by, and Monika's overhand form earned her the maximum score possible in every single one. All the while, Miranda continued using her standard form to match her.

Over time, public sentiment gradually began shifting Monika's way. That never-before-seen darts technique of hers had won over the audience. Miranda's throws were just as flawless, but their monotony caused the crowd to lose interest in her.

Each time Monika threw, cheers erupted from the crowd. The hall had regained its earlier fervor. But in the thirty-third round, the spectators grew more excited still.

"Look, at this rate, we're gonna be here for the rest of our lives," Monika said. She offered a proposal. "What do you say we start throwing all three darts at once?"

"Have you lost it?"

"What, too afraid? Look, it's easy."

The moment the words left her mouth, Monika clutched her three darts and hurled them all at once.

Once again, all of them found their mark, earning her another score of 180.

Monika had pulled off her biggest miracle yet, and it earned her a round of applause from the audience. She threw them a wave to stir them up even more.

Expectations were high for Miranda's next move—

"I'm here to play darts, not to do stunts."

—but she chose to stick to convention and throw her darts one at a time. It was the safer choice, and it got her a perfect score.

She was met with a storm of booing.

"Coward!" the crowd heckled her.

In the thirty-fourth, thirty-fifth, and thirty-sixth rounds, Monika continued overhand throwing all three darts at once, and the crowd kept roaring. In contrast, Miranda received nothing but unending jeers. "Quit being a chicken!" they shouted distractingly at her as she continued making her boring throws.

Not even Miranda was immune to conditions like those. Sweat began beading on her forehead, and Monika showed her no mercy. She went in for the kill.

Sara, now!

Sensing that Miranda's concentration was wavering, she flashed a hand signal.

A single mouse scurried underfoot, taking care to avoid the spectators' gazes. Then, the exact moment before Miranda made her throw, it leaped at her ankle.

Victory was Monika's. She was sure of it.

"Shoo!"

However, Miranda hadn't flinched.

Contrary to Monika's expectations, her third dart had landed right in the middle of the triple 20.

"........."

Monika gasped.

There was blood trickling down Miranda's heel. The mouse had sunk its teeth into her foot.

Yet, even so, she remained unfazed. Neither the booing nor Sara's surprise attack had thrown her off.

"You look surprised. Did you think you'd won?"

"........."

"It's no use," Miranda said as she readied her next dart. "I don't get shaken."

It was time for the thirty-seventh round. She carefully threw one dart, then the next.

"See, I've put in the hours. I've made tens of thousands of throws. Hundreds of thousands. No matter what you try to pull, all I have to do is believe in the hard work I've done."

The rhythm, speed, and trajectory of her throws hadn't changed a bit since the very first round. She was just making the exact same throw over and over, like a machine.

"Hard work, huh? You're saying that's the difference between you and me?"

Monika, on the other hand, was throwing all three of her darts at once and ending each of her rounds in the blink of an eye. It was a superhuman stunt that few, if any, could pull off.

The overtime rounds between their two diametrically opposed styles continued.

Now it was round thirty-eight.

"It is. And it's why *I* don't get tired." Miranda smiled. "I can see what you're up to, you know. You're not doing those three-in-one throws to show off. *You're doing it to cut down on the number of throws you need to make.* After all, that form of yours puts a lot of stress on your arm."

"………"

"Eventually, you'll slip. Not even prodigies are immune to fatigue."

She had Monika dead to rights there.

In order to get through the wind, Monika had to keep throwing her darts with all the power she could muster. Miranda, however, was able to continue casually using her by-the-book form. It went without saying which one of them would get worn out first.

The thirty-ninth round went by, as did the fortieth and forty-first.

"So?" Miranda asked. "Are you starting to feel it?"

"Hey, I'm sure you're getting worn out, too."

"I just told you, I don't *get* tired."

The forty-second, forty-third, and forty-fourth rounds passed as well.

"You could never understand just how long I've spent honing my craft. Me, getting worn out? Please. I could throw a thousand darts and never miss once."

"Why would you go so far?"

"Because of the pain."

"The what?"

"I can hear this man, talking in my head... **Keep training**, he says. And if I don't, the pain comes... *His* pain... The pain that feels like it'll split my heart in two... I have to keep throwing...no matter what it costs me... Now this is my life."

The forty-fifth round came and went.

"It's like being in hell... My body just moves on its own... I can't stand the pain. I can't do it... It's so scary, all I can do is cry... That's why I have to win..."

".........."

"And that's why I believe. I believe that if I just practice enough, I can overcome any adversity!"

After finishing her throw for the forty-sixth round, Monika exhaled. Their conversation just now had started to paint a picture for her—a picture of the puppet master secretly pulling the strings.

She massaged her throwing arm. There was only so long she could keep up the bravado. Just as Miranda had predicted, her exhaustion was starting to build. Being forced to repeatedly perform a motion she wasn't used to was causing her muscles to tighten. The situation was weighted against her, her opponent wasn't getting tired, and none of Monika's attempts to throw her off her game were working. It was becoming a war of attrition, and Monika was losing.

When the forty-seventh round rolled around, she had no choice but to change up her tactics. She raised just a single dart, having given up on throwing all three at once.

Miranda laughed mockingly. "Oh? Going back to throwing them one at a time?"

"Something like that."

"You must be scared that you're too tired to aim right. But upping your number of throws is a bad move, too, you know?"

Monika couldn't do her triple throw anymore because the risk she would flub it was too high. Given the war of attrition they were in, though, having to go back to performing three throws a round was a painful pill to swallow.

Monika grinned self-derisively.

Man, this would've been so much easier if I just had some poison on me the way Lily always does.

There was no point wishing for what she didn't have, but she had to admit, Lily could have turned the tables here with ease. Using poison gas that only she was immune to might have been foul play, but it certainly would've been enough to take down Miranda.

However, Monika had nothing of the sort.

She did technically have a special talent of her own: "creepshot," the ability she'd kept a secret from even her teammates. Her inhuman calculation skills and nigh-mechanical precision allowed her to track moving targets, either with or without the aid of mirrors.

It was a convenient skill for a spy to have…but at the end of the day, it was still just a technique. Monika didn't have an abnormal physiology or any sort of special ability stemming from a unique origin story. All she had was that single half-baked skill, and it wasn't even a particularly powerful one.

It's amazing I've made it this far with such a dog-shit ability, she thought sardonically as she continued doing her throws.

Their match continued on into the forty-eighth and forty-ninth rounds.

It was Monika's second throw in round fifty where disaster struck.

"Ah!"

The moment she released her dart, Monika's face contorted. She clutched at her arm.

Her dart flew up and to the right, eventually landing on the single 1. All she got for her efforts was one measly point.

"Looks like you finally hit your limit."

Meanwhile, Miranda's first two shots had both landed cleanly on the triple 20. As long as she made her third shot, Monika's defeat was a sure thing.

At the moment, their total scores had nearly reached nine thousand. There was no way Monika could come up with money like that.

Miranda smiled confidently and readied her third dart. "I'll remember this moment. It always feels fantastic when you surpass someone talented with nothing but hard work."

She was ready to settle the match.

A stir ran through the audience, and by chance, Monika spotted Sara's face among their ranks. She was standing on her tiptoes as high as she could go and mouthing a message to her.

"Miss Monika, you have to run!"

The logical part of Monika's brain realized that that would be the correct course of action. All she had to do was turn tail and flee. All she had to do was abandon her pride. The masked men in black suits had long since surrounded her, but there was still a chance she could break free.

However, Monika didn't move. She continued clutching her arm.

"Hard work alone isn't worth jack," she declared.

Miranda stopped mid-motion, and Monika went on.

"You've trained hard; I can't deny that. But on its own, that's not enough."

Miranda raised an eyebrow. "What're you going on about?"

"You piss me off, you know. You and those shitty values of yours."

"Excuse me?"

"What was it you said, *'if I just practice enough, I can overcome any adversity'*? What are you, stupid? How many people do you think have died in this world full of pain just because they were born in the wrong place and didn't have any talent?"

Monika was thinking of the man who called himself the World's Greatest.

He got it. He understood that sometimes things were just unfair, and no individual could overcome it. He knew about all the people who had died through no fault of their own. About the children who'd never even gotten so much as the opportunity to train. About the lives that had ended due to their bearers' lack of talent.

He'd explained as much back when they first met.

"You each have boundless potential just waiting to be unlocked."

That was the first thing he'd praised them for—their talent.

"There are walls in this world that no amount of effort is enough to get through."

It was simple, if you thought about it for a second.

If an average person trained and trained, would they ever be able to beat Klaus? The answer was a resounding no.

If you ever met him, you'd understand in an instant just how limited hard workers really are!

Monika had learned that all too well over these past few months. She clicked her tongue. "It's obnoxious, the way you pretend to be a nobody when you're just as talented yourself."

"Is that it? Was that pointless babbling your one final gambit?" Miranda laughed her off, then threw her dart. "Well, it's no use. That's game, set, and match!"

The moment it left her hand, Monika readied her dart in turn. "I'll tell you why you lost," she said. "It's your talent you should've trusted— not your effort."

Miranda had it all wrong.

The problem wasn't how she'd fallen for Monika's bait and thrown her third dart early. It was how steadfastly she'd clung to her hard work. That was what had led her to choose the same throw for her third dart as for all the others. She threw it from the same spot. At the same speed. With the same trajectory. If she'd changed up her throw even the tiniest amount, things would have been different. But using the exact same form against someone with Monika's adaptability was a careless mistake.

Monika threw her third dart with the exact same timing.

She wasn't aiming at the dartboard—she was aiming at Miranda's dart.

"What?"

Miranda shrieked.

Monika's exhaustion had all been an act. Her body still had some energy left, and she poured every last drop of it into her dart. It hurtled through the air at breakneck speed and sniped Miranda's dart right out of the air before bouncing off at an odd trajectory and spinning away.

As Monika watched it fly, she thought back.

There are hard limits to how far effort can get you...and normal people can never surpass prodigies.

Meeting Klaus had beaten that knowledge into her.

That was what happened when you went up against people who were on a whole different level.

But Klaus chose me. And he had the nerve to compliment me, even.

"*Magnificent.*"

He had said it on countless occasions, and each time, he had meant it.

I guess it's time for me to face the facts—the fact that I'm a prodigy, too.

When the chips were down, Monika had chosen to have faith in her own talents.

She had watched Miranda robotically perform the same throw 150 times in a row, and she had thought up a maneuver that bordered on impossible.

But Monika was confident that she could pull it off.

After knocking away Miranda's dart, Monika's dart spun through the air and landed exactly on target, striking the dartboard almost exactly where her first throw had landed.

"You're kidding me…"

"All that matters is where your darts land, right? Your words, not mine."

The fiftieth round was over.

Monika's final score was 8,901, and Miranda's was 8,900.

The crowd roared. The battle had raged for nearly two hours, and now at long last it had reached its conclusion. Over in the back, Sara gave her a teary round of applause.

Miranda crumpled to her knees.

Monika looked down at her. "I win."

"………"

"So? You gonna pay up? Or are you going to have to earn the money in one of those strip shows?"

Miranda's expression contorted.

Monika went on. "If that's not your cup of tea, I'd be happy to spot you the money. All you have to do is tell me who it is you're working for."

There was a puppet master behind the scenes who'd been feeding her orders and commanding her to take care of anyone who seemed even the slightest bit suspicious. If that puppet master happened to be Purple Ant, they could get tons of intel on him all at once.

She waited with high hopes for Miranda's response—

—until all of a sudden, Miranda plunged the tip of a dart into her own throat.

* * *

"……!" That was enough to shock even Monika. She grabbed Miranda by the arm. "What're you doing? There's no need for you to *die*."

"It's no use…" Miranda shook her head. "This is the rule…"

"What are you talking about?"

"*'If you lose, kill yourself,'* he said… If I don't, the pain will come… The punishment will come… I can't… I would rather die… My body won't listen to me anymore…" Miranda fought back against Monika's attempt to restrain her and continued trying to hasten along her suicide. Tears rolled down her cheeks, but she never stopped stabbing her throat. "I don't want to get punished…"

"___"

Monika could feel a rage welling up inside her. She finally understood what was really going on.

Miranda was a normal civilian. It was the puppet master's torture that had molded her into a soldier, nothing more. By nature, she was just a playful college student with a likable personality and a knack for darts.

Blood spewed from Miranda's throat as she mumbled deliriously. "…I wonder if the hero will come for me?"

"What?"

"Someone told me once that when I was in the depths of despair, a hero would show up and save me. Was it all just a lie? I can still hear their words echoing in my ears…"

It was like she was talking about something out of a children's story.

Realizing that Miranda wouldn't last much longer, Monika delivered a knife-hand strike to the back of her neck to knock her out. Even after she fell unconscious, though, her hand remained clasped tight around the dart as though duty bound.

"Get her some treatment," Monika barked at the casino workers. "You were in cahoots with her, right? If she tries to kill herself, make sure you stop her. I don't need my cut of the winnings."

However, that was little more than a stopgap. The moment Miranda woke up, she would go right back to her suicide attempt. There was no way to save her. No way, that was, except killing the puppet master.

Monika turned her back on the crowd and let out a low mutter. "Sara, let's go. We need to tell Intel about what we just saw."

"Yeah, you're right..."

The two of them left side by side and headed back aboveground.

Neither of them said another word until they were all the way to the top of the stairs.

They had won, but they didn't feel good about the way it had ended, and they hadn't even gained any actionable information. All they had to show for their efforts was the bad taste in their mouth from tormenting an innocent coed.

Monika whipped out her notepad, wrote down a coded message, and tore out the page, passing it to Sara. When she did, Sara retrieved the pigeon from beneath her hat and tied the note around his leg. The pigeon took flight and headed for the apartment where the Intel squad was staying.

"S-still, though!" Once they finished handling the report, Sara thoughtfully spoke up in a deliberately cheerful voice. "You were amazing back there, Miss Monika! It reminded me why I respect you so much!"

"Thanks. Your backup was pretty great, too."

"Oh, not at all! Honestly, I barely even did anything at—"

"You know, I really wish you'd start recognizing your own talent."

"......?"

"Still, you *did* save my butt this time around. Once we're done with this mission, I'm gonna give you some one-on-one coaching. Compared to the rest of Lamplight's pip-squeaks and numbskulls, you're one of the only people here with a decent head on your shoulders."

"R-really?" Sara's face reddened with joy.

Afterward, Monika took a dart out of her pocket and began twirling it around in her fingers.

Sara smiled. "Oh, you kept one?"

Monika nodded proudly. "Yeah, I thought this might be a good opportunity to start giving it a go."

"Wait...*start* giving it a go?"

"Yeah. That was a pretty good showing, right? Considering it was my first time playing and all."

Monika grinned as she watched Sara freeze with her mouth hanging agape.

* * *

The battle in the underground casino ended in victory for the Monika-Sara duo.

But a moment later, they were greeted by—

The Sybilla-Erna duo's battle was as fierce as could be.

Light had been entirely blocked out from the building, so all they could rely on were their nonvisual senses. However, their opponent, Barron, could traverse the darkness with ease. By listening for Sybilla's and Erna's breathing, he could gauge how far away they were. Moving around silently to take down his target seemed to be a core tenet of his fighting style.

He took care not to let them sense his hostility, then closed in on them and lashed out with his trained boxer's fist. A single direct hit would be enough to put them out like a light.

The only tools they had to fight back with were Sybilla's physical prowess—

"He's coming from the left!"

—and Erna's incredible intuition.

Sybilla reacted to her call by immediately stooping down and throwing out a kick. When her foot made contact, it gave her a decent idea of where her opponent was, and she fired her gun without a moment's hesitation. During the brief moment her muzzle flash lit up the darkness, she caught a glimpse of Barron's face.

He had assumed he had his prey cornered, and he was none too happy about her sudden counterattack.

"You little worm," he spat.

Sybilla hadn't been able to see her target, so she had failed to deal him a fatal blow. Barron beat a hasty retreat, his footsteps echoing out as he vanished into the darkness once more.

Sybilla nudged Erna behind her back and angled herself so that Erna was sandwiched between her and the wall. There was no need for them to change up their position. Either way, Barron would have no trouble tracking them down.

The deadly clash in the darkness reached a momentary lull.

"Erna, lemme pick your brain for a sec," Sybilla said. "What do you think we can do to get the upper hand?"

Whenever things started to go off book, Sybilla knew that deferring to her teammates was a better call than relying on her own judgment. Erna might not be on Grete's level, but she was still pretty good when it came to thinking on her feet.

Barron could hear them, too, but there was no getting around that. Given how sharp his ears were, even whispering probably wouldn't have made a difference.

Erna gave her reply instantly. "For now, we have to fall back." The situation was dire enough that nobody would have blamed her for flying into a panic, but she laid out her thought process with utmost composure. "The entrance we came through is blocked, so we'll have to use another exit, but fighting in here puts us at too big of a disadvantage."

"It stings, but I guess you're right. As things are, I'm not seein' any way we win."

"Don't think of it as losing. Think of it as retreating so we can win later."

"Ooh, I like the sound of that. One question, though—"

"Hmm?"

"—which way's the exit?"

"...................................."

Without their sight, they had no way of figuring out an escape route. Neither of them had ever been in the building before, and they'd been forced to rush about so haphazardly that they had no idea where exactly they were.

Behind her, Erna groaned. "How unlucky..."

"Yeah, well, them's the breaks."

For now, it looked like they had no choice but to continue fighting in the dark. Given their current situation, fumbling around blindly was too dangerous to be a legitimate option. They would have no way to tell from which direction Barron was going to attack them.

Erna spoke up again. "He's coming from straight ahead!"

Sybilla took a guess at when Barron would strike, then slid along the wall and used the slight variations in airflow to aim her shot. Their lack of sight made the sound of her gunshot seem that much louder. This time, though, her bullet failed to find its mark. And when it did, Barron's fist came hurtling through the darkness!

It took everything Sybilla had just to stop the blow. She blocked the jab-hook combo with her arm, then let Erna tug her away.

Barron's voice echoed eerily through the dark. "*Oui.* You're a perceptive one."

Sybilla couldn't feel the arm she'd blocked with. She could tell she'd suffered some internal bleeding. She fired a defensive shot, and Barron backed off again. It was classic hit-and-run tactics. Back during his time as a professional, he might well have been an out-boxer.

This time, he didn't waste a moment before coming in for another attack, and Erna's warning only barely came in time. If Sybilla hadn't also heard Barron's shoes scrape the ground, she would've been done for. She dodged the blow to her face by a hairbreadth and had to practically crawl across the ground to make her escape.

I'm not gonna last much longer like this!

Barron would've been a nasty opponent to fight in close quarters at the best of times, and even with Erna's intuition to help, battling him in the dark was a recipe for taking a one-sided beatdown. Plus, escaping would be even harder once she ran out of bullets.

"Yeep...," she heard Erna worriedly mumble.

Sybilla reached out in the dark and joined hands with her, then followed her lead as she rushed out of the room. Shortly thereafter, Erna crashed headlong into a wall. Sybilla quickly put her back to it and got ready to defend herself from Barron again.

"Hey, Barron!" she shouted, no longer able to hold herself back.

The response came from somewhere in the darkness. "...*Oui?*"

Sybilla briefly considered firing a shot in the direction the voice came from, but she knew she couldn't waste her precious bullets on gut reads.

"Why're you doin' this?" Instead, she decided to ask him a question. "You coulda kept makin' it as a boxer, no? Why get involved with this assassination crap?"

The way the VP told it, he had been forced into retirement by an injury, but that clearly wasn't the real story. It was obvious from looking at him that he was still in his prime.

"*Oui.* Why should I tell you?" he replied curtly.

"Eh, have it your way."

As Sybilla shrugged, she heard Barron sigh. "Besides," he went on. "You're the same. Neither of us can live out in the sun."

There was a certain heaviness to his tone.

"People like us have nowhere we can go. All we can do is scuttle about in the dark. Am I wrong?"

His voice rang with a resigned determination.

Sybilla hadn't had high hopes, and sure enough, talking him down wasn't going to be an option. She had no choice but to fight.

The sound of Barron's breathing vanished, as though to say that the time for talk was over. He slipped back under the cover of darkness and got ready to launch another attack.

Sybilla braced herself.

For a moment, everything was silent. Combined with their inability to see, the total lack of sound made it feel as though the world itself had ended. None of the light from Main Street's dazzling billboards or the raucous sound of its gridlocked car horns could reach them there.

"He's coming...from the right?" Erna whispered. Her intonation was a touch different than it had been the other times.

Sybilla could sense that something was up, too.

Their foe was mixing up his attack pattern. She could still sense the punch coming her way, but something about it was different. After focusing every nerve in her body, Sybilla realized what had changed. Barron wasn't going after her this time—he was going after Erna.

Instead of targeting the athletic Sybilla, he had decided to attack the weaker member of the duo.

He silently swooped past Sybilla and bore down on her partner—

"Oh, no, you don't!"

—but Sybilla reacted by firing off a beautiful backspin kick.

It was a feat that demanded extraordinary reflexes, but that was precisely what Sybilla had.

Her attack had been a complete shot in the dark, but she felt it land solidly on Barron's face. Her body had moved on its own this time, and that was what had made the difference.

"You're not layin' one goddamn finger on my girl!"

It was a critical hit.

She still couldn't see Barron, but at long last, she'd landed a blow on him.

The problem was—

"*Oui.* What a child, falling for bait that simple."

—her foe had seen it all coming.

Barron had been planning on taking Sybilla's attack from the get-go. He caught the leg that had slammed into his face and threw her off-balance.

Sybilla immediately grabbed at him.

Barron sank his fist into her exposed abdomen. "It's over."

The punch landed right in her solar plexus. She couldn't breathe, and her mind went blank.

Before she knew it, she had already fallen to the ground and landed hard. She tumbled across the dusty floor. By the time she finally came to a stop, she couldn't lift her arms or legs anymore.

"Big Sis Sybilla…?"

Erna sounded grief-stricken.

"Nah, I'm good," Sybilla replied, fighting through the pain to raise Erna's spirits. She smiled. "Check out what I just nicked."

And in the darkness, there was light.

A tiny flame lit up the room. Everything came into view—the abandoned desks, Erna's widened eyes, and Barron, who was staring at Sybilla in shock.

She was holding a lighter.

"You little…," Barron growled.

Sybilla had remembered everything. She had remembered the lighter Barron had used to light the VP's cigarette, and she had remembered exactly which pocket he put it into afterward.

She squinted and used the dim light to look around. There was a map hanging on the wall.

There's the exit!

They didn't have time to dawdle. If the lighter ran out of fuel, they'd be done for.

Sybilla summoned up her strength and rose back to her feet. Then she grabbed Erna by the arm and made a break for it.

Barron watched calmly as the two girls fled, then gave chase. However, he didn't run at full throttle. He tracked them by the light from the lighter they were holding, but he made no efforts to close the distance.

"Time for us to get the hell out of here!" the girl called Sybilla cheered.

Her voice was spirited. She was confident that she'd won. Once she escaped from the darkness, she'd have a chance to gather her bearings and prepare for round two.

The thing is..., Barron thought to himself as he continued feigning agony. *You won't be going anywhere.*

At the end of the day, he had nothing to fear from shallow-minded children like them. Everything was still going *exactly according to his plan.*

You were too conspicuous. You ended up showing me everything.

It had happened by pure coincidence, but Barron had spotted her.

When he saw an apprentice journalist doggedly covering suspicious politicians, he immediately put his guard up. Then he used her personality to infer how she operated. By the time she approached the VP he worked for, he already had a pretty solid idea about how good of a pickpocket she was.

That information had let him devise the perfect plan.

The fact that you're a hothead let me predict you'd come charging at me, and the first thing you'd go for would be my lighter. It's the obvious choice to make for a person trapped in the dark.

Barron watched Sybilla run off, lighter in hand.

And when you spotted that map, you'd have no reason not to follow it.

She wasn't unskilled, not by any stretch of the imagination. Barron had no doubt that she'd trained to be able to commit things to memory within an instant of seeing them. Unfortunately for her, though, she lacked the prudence to pair with her talents.

The map had directions to a set of stairs leading to the fifth floor. All you have to do is take a left at the fire extinguisher and go straight past the break room, and you'll arrive at the fire escape.

Barron squeezed his fists tight.

But that fire escape is where I laid my trap!

Any foot they set on those stairs would get hacked up by the piano wire he'd strung across them. From there, they would be helpless to resist as gravity and inertia carried them down and the piano wire sliced them to ribbons.

Then he could hunt them down at his leisure.

Barron's foes tended to be wary of his combat prowess and his sharp ears, but his true weapon was his craftiness. Whenever he went after someone, he made sure to carefully back them into a corner, then lure them into his traps without ever relinquishing the advantage.

"*Oui*... Get back here...," he shouted after them threateningly. He pretended to be out of breath, like he couldn't possibly catch them.

"No thanks!" Sybilla shouted back.

Barron quietly gloated. *Perfect.*

Scrabble and claw your way to the light. Flee the darkness as fast as you can.

If anything, it wasn't Sybilla he was worried about—it was the younger one. With senses as sharp as hers, there was an outside chance she might figure out the piano wire trap. However, Barron had already seen that when he put the pressure on, those abilities of hers were greatly diminished.

"Big Sis Sybilla, we need to hurry..."

Sure enough, there was sweat gushing from the younger girl's brow as she used the lighter's flame to guide her. There was no way she'd be able to make unclouded decisions in a situation so relentlessly stressful.

Battling to the death in the dark was a nerve-racking experience. It tended to make people act hastily.

Barron's victory was assured.

You two will never escape this darkness. Your lives will end in this prison I've built.

His eyes widened with amusement.

This here is the end of the line!

A few more yards, and they'd be able to reach the fire escape.

The two girls charged down the hallway, and the moment they reached the corner with the fire extinguisher—

"Nah, this ain't right."

—Sybilla stopped in her tracks.

It was unthinkable. Why would she stop when she was so close to freedom?

"What's going on?" Barron muttered.

They hadn't reached the stairs yet, so there was no way she could've noticed his trap. And he hadn't heard her partner say anything, either. She, too, looked up at Sybilla in surprise. "Yeep?"

Sybilla stripped off her jacket, tossed it to the floor, and hurled the still-lit lighter at it. The jacket caught fire and began burning in seconds.

"With this much fire, we can get in a good three minutes of fighting. That's plenty of time for either of us, right?"

The flame's light lit up her face, revealing the fearless grin she was wearing.

Barron's eyes went wide.

Why would she stop there? When the fire dies out, she'll be plunged back into darkness again...

He couldn't for the life of him figure out what had inspired her change of heart. Instead of trying to advance some tactic, he simply asked the first question that came to mind. "Aren't you afraid of the dark?"

"Why would I be? I'm not some kid." Sybilla laughed mockingly. "Nah, runnin' away's just a little too cowardly for my tastes. And I don't need this gun, either. Let's settle this thing mano a mano."

"Wh—?!"

Barron *really* hadn't seen that one coming.

Sybilla fished her gun out of her pocket and tossed it over by her teammate. She even dropped her knife on the floor with a dry *thump*.

I don't get it... Why would she go and do something so illogical?

Barron's heart began racing. His body heated up, and he was sweating from every pore.

All his calculations were falling apart. He thought he had his opponent trapped in the palm of his hand, but she'd broken free and become something he couldn't comprehend.

Calling something "cowardly" when we're fighting to the death? What does she think this is, some sort of sporting match?

Barron was under no obligation to rise to her challenge. He had a gun. He could just shoot her. The only reason he hadn't done so already was because not even he was any good at aiming in the dark.

By the time he reached into his jacket, Sybilla had already closed the gap. "Y'know what I think?!" She slammed her fists into him. "I think you've been stressed as hell this whole time. It's like you can barely even breathe!"

From the way she sounded, it was like she actually *enjoyed* fighting.

Barron couldn't even begin to understand her. Her movements were keen and nimble, and she threw out combinations of punches and low kicks without pause.

"Breathing...is overrated...," Barron groaned as he weathered her attacks.

He was thinking of the violence that man had wrought.

Barron had been enjoying a nice Christmas get-together with his family when the man and his henchmen showed up. Before he knew what was going on or why they had come, the men dragged them off and subjected them to horrible pain. Barron was powerless to do anything but watch as the people he loved screamed.

"Have you ever had to listen to your son wailing his lungs out? To your wife pleading for her life? You could never understand the agony of hearing your family suffer or know how that pain burns its way into your brain..."

After ten hours of that—after it had worn his soul ragged—the man had whispered to him.

"Become my Worker Ant and kill spies for me."

Barron had had no choice but to obey. His body moved on its own. He had been reduced to nothing more than the man's puppet. He killed without hesitation, taking his years of boxing experience and using them to learn how to assassinate people.

"I'll kill you... I'll kill you and save my family..."

Close-quarters combat? Bring it on.

He evaded Sybilla's attack, then took advantage of his larger build to leap at her like he was trying to smother her. They each grabbed the other's shoulders and began grappling for control.

There was no way Barron was going to lose in a battle of raw power. Sybilla might have been strong for a girl, but she was no match for him. He began pushing her backward. Once he had her up against the wall, he could strangle her.

"Family, huh?"

Yet, even so, her smile refused to fade.

"I get that. I wanted to save my family, too. I wanted to save my kid brother and kid sister."

"Then why…are you smiling…?"

"Outta regret. I charged forward like an idiot, and all I did was mess everything up. I tried squeezin' what little brains I had for all they were worth, and I still couldn't see shit. I'm tellin' you, man, it felt hopeless. Like I didn't have a future."

Her eyes shone, piercing and true.

"But then, there was this guy who said I was *'magnificent.'*"

"………"

"Those words gave me a little shot of hope. And now? Hell, now I'm a goddamn optimist."

Barron couldn't relate to a word she was saying. All he'd been given was a set of orders by a mysterious man.

"Kill them all."

"If you lose, kill yourself."

"If you don't, your family is done for."

Barron had been killing for three long years.

He'd trained in the art of espionage, he'd studied how to extract information from people, he'd learned the exact angle it took to snap someone's neck in close-quarters combat, and he'd mastered the technique of relying on sound to move about in absolute darkness. And yet, once every month, his phone would ring, and he would hear his wife and son screaming through the receiver.

"Then you and that happy-go-lucky brain of yours can die here," he shot back, "and be forgotten in the darkness."

"You're wrong, you know. I can go anywhere I damn well please."

Barron shoved her against the wall as though trying to rebut her remark. "You're finished."

He reached for her slender neck.

Then he saw a head of blond hair flit across the corner of his vision.

He let go of Sybilla on reflex. The moment he did, a thunderous roar split the air, and a bullet grazed his face. The bullet was massive—the mere airflow from it passing by was enough to make his face go hot.

After whizzing past him, it sank deep into the wall.

Was that a magnum round? That's a big gun she must've used…

Barron took another look at the blond girl.

The recoil from the shot had been too much for her, and she was in the middle of tumbling over backward. The gun she'd used was much too large for her petite frame. She rolled away helplessly and hit her head hard on the wall.

"Yeep!" she groaned. Then she mumbled, "How unlucky...," and passed out.

Barron hadn't even needed to waste any time on her.

She had been a mystery to him from start to finish, but once he killed her, that would be that.

He turned back toward Sybilla. "All right, it's high time I finished th—"

But before he could complete his sentence, a gunshot rang out.

"What...?"

His legs gave out under him, and he crumpled to the ground.

The next thing he felt was a sharp pain in his knee.

He'd been shot.

Barron looked up in blank shock. There, he saw Sybilla holding his automatic.

"You shot me...?"

She must have nabbed it during the brief moment the blond girl stole his attention.

The problem was, it didn't make sense. Sybilla herself was the one who had wanted to fight mano a mano. Why go back to using a gun?

"I—I thought you said you didn't like cowardly tactics?"

"What? We're spies fighting to the death. There ain't no rules here. That was just some bullshit I fed you to get you to lower your guard," she responded flatly. "I didn't *mean* it."

Everything she was saying was totally logical. However, the contrast between her words and her actions was still throwing him off. "Then... Then why not just flee through the fire escape?!"

Earlier, Sybilla had stopped in her tracks and chosen to fight him fair and square instead of escaping out of the darkness. If she didn't have a problem with using cowardly tactics, she could have just fled down the fire escape in the first place. Her behavior was inconsistent. Barron couldn't make heads or tails of it.

"It doesn't make sense. You saw the map, so you could've gotten down from the sixth floor. Why hesitate?"

Sybilla grinned like she'd just figured out what he was talking about. "Ah, I see. So that's why your plan fell apart. I take it you rigged the stairs with a trap or somethin'?"

"........."

"Looks like I was right about how stressed out you were. The answer was dead simple, and you couldn't even see it."

"I missed something...?"

Barron had been observing Sybilla, and he'd watched her working as a journalist as he devised his plan for how to kill her. What was it he'd overlooked?

Everything he'd seen and heard flashed back through his mind.

"Do your comments from this morning contradict the department meeting minutes that got published yesterday or what?"

"Excuse me?! Wh-what are you on about?!"

"Here, try something from this menu next."

"For real? You're a lifesaver, man. In that case, I'll go for this one here, third from the top on the left."

Realizing the truth took Barron's breath away.

It was impossible. It was utterly unthinkable, and here she was, casually confessing to it.

"Don't tell me you seriously can't..."

"Look, I studied my ass off on the boat ride over here. But I'm tellin' ya, this Mouzaia language is a doozy. There just wasn't enough time. I learned how to speak it, but that's as far as I got." She stuck out her tongue. "As far as written stuff goes, *I can't read a word of it.*"

It finally made sense. That was why she'd given up on fleeing—she simply hadn't been able to read the map. The words *fire extinguisher, break room,* and *fire escape* had meant nothing to her. She had just picked a direction and run. She hadn't had the first clue where the fire escape actually was.

But how could he have predicted that?

What kind of spy infiltrated a country without even learning its language?!

It was like she wasn't even taking her job seriously. Still, though, it was a possibility Barron had overlooked, and as a result, he ended up dancing to her rhythm. The moment things went off plan, she had stolen the initiative from him at every turn.

Well…I guess I lost.

The bleeding from his knee wasn't stopping. She'd punctured an artery. He hurriedly tried to stop up the wound, but in the back of his mind, he still remembered the man's order, and he still remembered the pain.

"If you lose, kill yourself."

Barron's body refused to move. His brain had been thoroughly trained, and it had no interest in stopping the bleeding. It wanted him to end his life.

However, he knew that if he died, his wife and son would be killed. He had no illusions about a man that cruel having an ounce of mercy in his body.

I want to live… I don't want to die… I want to see my family again…

He searched for hope. He wanted so badly to find a light in that darkness.

The blood loss was making everything feel hazy. It wouldn't be long before he bled to death.

I can hear a voice. What's going on? Who was it who told me this?

"A hero is coming. They'll show up and save you when you're at your darkest hour."

"You have to make sure you survive until they get here."

He could no longer remember who it was who had said that to him, but he remembered their voice being warm—the exact opposite of that cruel man's. However, it was all a lie. He was reaching out to be saved, but no one was coming.

There was no hero in Mitario.

◇◇◇

Sybilla muttered incoherently to herself as she watched Barron slip into unconsciousness.

The hell's goin' on with this guy? He didn't even try to stanch his own wound...

Her goal had never been to kill him. After all, she needed to pump him for information on the puppet master. However, he had let his blood run freely and passed out. At this rate, Barron was going to die.

Sybilla was under no obligation to save him, of course, but still...

"God*dammit!*" she shouted as she began administering emergency first aid.

The bullet had passed clean through, so he was losing a lot of blood, but there was still a chance she could save him. She bound his wounded knee up tight to stop the bleeding. All she needed to do now was get out of the building and call an ambulance.

She just hoped he'd be able to hold on until then. It was pretty obvious from what he'd been saying that someone had been manipulating him, and Sybilla doubted that he deserved to die.

Erna was still conked out with a lump on her head, so Sybilla had to go wake her up before quietly escaping from the sixth floor. Sure enough, the fire escape connecting to the fifth floor was filled with traps, so they had to disarm them before heading down.

"Well, I can't say it feels great, but a win's a win," Sybilla remarked.

"Yeah."

Sybilla wrote up a report as they walked, then tied it to the mouse Erna had brought with her. The mouse was Sara's, and it had been trained to carry messages to the Intel squad.

Side by side, the two of them rushed out into the open. They could see the lights from the other buildings now. In unison, they sucked in big breaths and drew oxygen into their lungs. Then, upon realizing how they'd both done the exact same thing, they burst into laughter.

"Y'know, we make a pretty damn good team."

"I feel like I can do anything when I'm with you, Big Sis Sybilla."

After complimenting each other's efforts, they exchanged a light fist bump.

Sybilla scratched her cheek bashfully. "Big Sis, huh..."

She still hadn't told the rest of her team about her family. She hadn't told them about how her dad had run a gang, how she was the one who'd turned him in to the cops, or how she and her siblings had fled to an orphanage. Or how...

She shook her head.

"I like it! Don't you worry about a thing; your big sis has got your back!"

Visions of the past overlaid with the present, and Sybilla gave Erna a lighthearted smile.

The battle in the multi-tenant building ended in victory for the Sybilla-Erna duo.

But a moment later, they ran into—

A pair of small creatures showed up at Thea and Grete's window.

It was a mouse and a pigeon, both of which belonged to Sara. The critters were Lamplight's primary means of communication. Radios and telephones could both be tapped, so save for emergencies, they passed their messages to one another via animals.

The fact that they'd just shown up meant that Monika and Sybilla had successfully made it out of danger. Thea breathed a sigh of relief and let in the two animals, and Grete wasted no time in reading the notes strapped to them and passing the information along to Thea.

She told her about the darts game in the underground casino and the battle in the darkened building. Then she went on to describe how the others had overcome their still unidentified foe.

"...and there you have it," she finished.

Thea couldn't help but let out another sigh. "That's incredible," she replied. "They really did it. They defeated their opponents!"

They were in a foreign land with no idea what their enemy even looked like, and the girls had defeated their foes all on their own. Thea was overwhelmed at how quickly her teammates were improving.

"...Just as I expected." Grete nodded calmly. "Monika and Sybilla both have tremendous physical abilities at their disposal. With Sara and Erna there to provide backup, I knew they would be able to overcome nearly any obstacle."

"Y-yeah, you're right. I suppose I shouldn't be surprised."

"Still, they've lived up to my expectations wonderfully."

"........."

What surprised Thea wasn't just the fantastic result the Operations and Specialist squads had just put up. It was the fact that *Grete had seen it all coming.* By and large, she was the one who'd decided where to deploy the field teams. Assassins had come after them just like Grete wanted, and because the Specialist squad members had been able to run interference, Lamplight had succeeded in turning the tables on its foes. The way she'd assigned them to their locations and considered the synergy between each respective duo was nothing short of impeccable.

You know, I always thought that Monika stood head and shoulders above all the rest of us, but now...

Now Thea realized how wrong she'd been. As it turned out, there was another girl on the team whose talents were similarly outsized.

Grete hadn't been nearly so skilled back when Thea first met her. She had been resourceful, sure, but between her frail physique and her androphobia, it had come as little surprise that she had washed out of her academy.

Something must have triggered that change.

Something...like having an encounter so intense it had turned her entire worldview on its head.

As Thea sat there struck utterly speechless, Grete remained totally on the ball. "I am still worried about Lily, though. We should send the others over to rendezvous with her. There's still so little we actually know, and if we don't brace ourselves for the unexpected, things could quickly take a turn for the worse."

"Y-you're totally right. I'll get in touch with them via radio."

"You should make sure to loop in the boss, too, if you can get ahold of him."

Thea headed over to the radio setup sitting in the corner of the room. She was relieved that her friends were okay, but that was only one of the emotions swirling around in her heart.

It's almost funny how pathetic I am...

Her teammates were out risking their lives, and here she was sitting pretty in her safe apartment and doing nothing but following Grete's instructions.

It was a sorry state of affairs. She bit down on her lip and got to work operating the radio.

For now, though, I have to do what needs doing. It's best I just keep my head down and make sure I don't get in Grete's way.

There were no options remaining to her. The others had all advanced their skills and left her in the dust, and this was the only part she could play.

The moment she went to turn on the radio, the telephone in the center of the room began ringing.

"We're getting a call?" Her fingers froze. "From whom? Whoever it is, it must be urgent."

Grete gave the phone a quizzical look as well. Maybe someone had new intel. Thea stopped reaching for the radio and picked up the receiver instead. She was immediately greeted by a sunny voice.

"Yo, it's me."

It was Annette. Last they had heard, she was with Lily.

"Wh-what's going on?" Thea asked.

"I'll make it brief. The cops were on our heels, so me and Flower Garden had to run around for a while. We ran into a biiit of a kerfuffle, but I ended up getting away."

"Well, that's good to hear."

It sounded like those two had overcome their trial as well. If whatever kerfuffle they'd run into was minor enough that they were able to get away, then all was well that ended well. Annette and Lily's teamwork must have been pretty impressive, too.

But if that was the case, then why the phone call?

The next words Thea heard sounded almost unsettlingly cheerful.

"That was when a dozen assassins came after us, yo."

"A dozen?!"

Thea yelped with shock, and Grete, who was listening beside her, did as well.

According to the reports, their assailants had been formidable enough that it had taken two girls apiece to defeat each of them, and even then, the fights had been dangerously close. Securing victory had required surviving more than a few brushes with death. Going up against twelve opponents like that at once would be a one-way ticket to the slaughterhouse.

"*So how long are we gonna have to keep them busy for, yo?*"

"W-wait, back up a few steps. You're safe now, right? Where's Lily?" Thea asked, unable to stop herself from accidentally referring to Lily by her actual name.

Annette's reply came promptly. "*She distracted them so I could get away. Now she's buying time.*"

"She did *what*...?"

"*The thing is, she's not gonna last long.*"

Lily was fighting all on her own.

She had entrusted the intel to Annette, and now she was putting her life on the line to stall their foes.

"I-I'll send the others to you right away! Just make sure you survive until they get to—"

"*Nah, see, that's what she wanted me to tell you,*" Annette said. "*There's a good chance the same thing is happening to the others, too.*"

The radio buzzed.

That was their emergency distress signal—the way their teammates could call for help if they needed it badly enough to be willing to risk their message getting intercepted.

Two of its lights were lit up. One was white; the other was blue.

"Thea...," Grete murmured, "those are SOS calls from Sybilla and Monika..."

That was enough to make Thea go as pale as a sheet. Now she finally understood the score. They had gone up against an opponent they were wildly underequipped to handle.

Who were these people who were willing to sacrifice everything else in their lives to train, who carried out orders from above without hesitating, who tried to kill themselves when they lost, and who had their allies come in afterward to crush their foes with sheer numbers? The only way someone could do all that was by throwing away their sense of self altogether.

It was like they were soldiers. No, it was more than that—it was like they were *ants*, willing to throw away their very lives to serve their regent.

Was that Purple Ant's power?

If a dozen assassins were arriving at three places at once, that meant that there had to be at least thirty-six of them. It boggled the mind. If there really were that many, it was cause for despair. Lamplight had no chance against numbers like that.

Just how many people were they up against?

Thea started running the numbers on just how much danger they were in. She needed to figure out how deep their opponent's roster went.

Were there thirty of them? Forty? Or worst of all...*fifty*?

Interlude

Purple Ant ③

"Two hundred and eighty-seven—that's how many Worker Ants I have in Mitario," said Purple Ant. The number fluctuated from time to time, but that was generally about where he kept it.

If you included the Worker Ants he had scattered across the globe, their full ranks were more than four hundred strong.

"I have them deployed all across the city. Their orders are to kill any spy they find, and if they fail, another twelve of them will come in to finish the job."

As he spoke, he split peanut shells between his fingers, removed the peanuts from within, and lined them up on his so-called pet dog's back. Once he had 287 of them in neat little rows, he nodded in satisfaction.

His captive still wasn't saying much, so he had decided to handle the exposition himself.

At the moment, he was in the middle of explaining his devastating ability. He wasn't worried in the slightest about her doing anything with the information. After all, her fate was already sealed. "No spy can compete with numbers like that. And even if someone managed to capture a Worker Ant, the majority of them are under orders to kill themselves the moment they're beaten. Your people put up a good fight, but alas, those minor skirmishes you won meant nothing."

His captive shot him a quizzical look. In her eyes, something didn't add up.

"I know what you're wondering," Purple Ant said understandingly. "You're thinking that if my Worker Ants banded together, they could take me down. Is that it?"

She nodded.

It was a legitimate thought. If one of those groups of twelve Worker Ants teamed up and conspired to kill him, it would pose a serious threat to his life.

"Well, you're absolutely right. As a matter of fact, even the bartender or my pet dog here could kill me like it was nothing. I'm no good at fighting myself, you see. Oh, dearie me! If they turn on me now, I'm done for!"

Those two had exceptional skills, even for Worker Ants.

If either of them ever wanted to kill him, it would take them only a few seconds to finish the deed. All they would need to do was crush his throat with their bare hands, and freedom would be theirs.

But that was something they'd never be able to do.

"The mere thought of it is ridiculous. You'd do well not to take my power so lightly." Purple Ant kicked the dog man in the stomach. **"Strangle yourself."**

The moment the words left his mouth, the dog reached up and began squeezing his own neck. His fingers dug into his flesh. He started letting out pained gasps, but he still didn't loosen his grip.

Purple Ant watched with clear amusement as the dog man got to work killing himself. "And there you have it. They can't rise against me, not with how I've wired their minds. The revolution will never come. They'll just keep on obeying my orders until the day their meaningless lives end."

Right before the man passed out, Purple Ant stopped him. **"That's enough."** He cruelly dug his foot into his exhausted "pet."

"That's why nobody can beat me."

His captive was still unable to speak—even more so now.

Purple Ant proudly listed off his accomplishments. "I wiped out the CIM's Retias team. The five of them managed to kill fourteen Worker Ants, but that was as far as they went. Now, the Goosefoot Sisters were smart. They ran for it after their seventh kill. The older sister didn't make it, but still. Shadowseed committed suicide after nine kills. The JJJ started sniffing around my business, too, but that ended quickly when I sent them the Giraffe's and the Turtle's corpses. And Ouka, Ouka was incredible. He managed to kill seventeen of my Worker Ants all on his own. I have to say, seeing his corpse gave me a shock. I had no idea he was just a teenage boy."

White Spider had described them as international all-stars, but they had all been powerless against Purple Ant. He had an inexhaustible supply of assassins who cared nothing for their own lives. Even if his foes tried to capture one, his minions would just kill themselves without a moment's hesitation. Then the next assassin would descend.

Purple Ant's position was nigh unassailable.

He had the power to crush every spy who entered his territory and every member of the secret police trying to defend it, and what's more, he could do it all without having to lift a finger.

"Also, I've already gotten started replacing the Worker Ants I've lost. It's simple, really. All I have to do is track down promising civilians so I can capture and torment them."

And thus, his reign would continue.

There wasn't a single person in all of Mitario who could stand up to him.

"How many…?"

He heard a hoarse voice.

His prisoner was finally choosing to speak, glaring at him with all her might.

"How many lives do you have to ruin before you're satis—?"

"Don't talk back to the king." Purple Ant kicked her.

He was halfway through pummeling her face before he finally returned to his senses.

"Ah, I'm so sorry. It's a policy of mine to be kind to women, yet here I am, resorting to violence…" He apologetically removed his hat and offered her a smile. "Let's all see if we can't mind our manners, shall we?"

Purple Ant thought of himself as a gentleman, and it was a designation he'd never once doubted. After all, every time he hit a woman, it filled him with remorse. Oh, what a compassionate king he was. And so humble!

The question was, why had he hit her?

One reason was because of how much of an eyesore his dog was. He gave the man another kick to the stomach as punishment for that transgression.

The other reason was because the man he was waiting for was nowhere to be seen. He glanced down at his watch. Quite a bit of time had already passed.

"Unfortunate. Young Klaus doesn't seem to be coming, does he? You'd think he would have at least killed one of the Worker Ants by now."

Purple Ant hadn't received a single report of anyone having seen him.

According to his intel, Klaus treasured his allies, so Purple Ant had been working under the assumption that if he kidnapped a Din spy, Klaus would be sure to show up.

Where was he? Had he abandoned his teammate to her fate?

Purple Ant's patience was wearing thin.

"Oh, forget this. I'll just kill you now."

He pulled out his automatic and blasted his captive right in the gut.

The sound of the shot rang out loud.

Fresh blood splattered across the bar, and a metallic smell filled the room.

"With that, I'd say you have about five minutes before you bleed out," Purple Ant said. "If you have any dying words, I would love to hear them. But first, there's one matter that still needs settling."

He wiped away the blood that had splashed on his face and went on.

"Now, before you die…would you be so kind as to finally tell me your name?"

Chapter 4

Peril

Crises befell all three locations at almost exactly the same time.

It was 2300 hours. The dead of night.

As the buildings and billboards gleamed over on Main Street, people began leaving the side streets in droves. Mitario might have been the biggest metropolis on the globe, but the seediness of its underbelly was world-class as well. Law-abiding citizens did their best to avoid walking down back alleys at night.

The only people who went there were those who preferred to operate away from prying eyes.

It was those very alleys that the girls raced through.

One of the alleyways sat to the northwest of the station.

After securing their victory in the underground casino, Monika and Sara got attacked again. A sniper shot whizzed through the air as they made their way back to Main Street. All the bullet did was graze Monika's leg, but it told them that they needed to run.

The aftertaste from their win left their mouths in a hurry as they found themselves back in combat.

The two of them moved in tandem and fled away from Main Street.

As they ran through the alleys, though, it suddenly dawned on them that there was far more than one sniper. Monika hurled her mirrors to try and figure out how many of them there were, and the ultimate count she settled on was twelve. Their foes were racing across rooftops and creeping along alleyway walls as they chased the two of them down.

Before the Lamplight duo realized it, they'd been lured into the snipers' hunting grounds. They were trapped alongside a river with nowhere to run.

Not even Monika had gone and memorized the exact layout of every alleyway in Mitario. Their foes probably lived in the area, and they'd used their knowledge of the terrain to devastating effect.

When Monika and Sara finally broke away, they dove inside a nearby building and took a moment to catch their breaths. It was a tailor shop, and the workers had already gone home for the day. The two girls hid themselves behind the counter.

"Well, this doesn't look great for us," Monika said with a hint of worry in her smile.

Their foes were checking every building in the area one by one. It was only a matter of time before they rooted her and Sara out.

So, Miranda was basically just the scouting party...

Their opponents were far stronger than she'd given them credit for.

"M-Miss Monika...!" Sara said with tears in her eyes. "You could've gotten away if it was just you, right? The only reason you're stuck here is because you had to protect me!"

"Is it? I dunno what you're talking about."

"I-if we're both going to die here, then it would be better if you just made a break for it on your own..."

"............"

After a long silence, Monika grinned self-mockingly. "If I did that, it'd make a *certain someone* real sad."

"What...?"

"Hey, don't ask me. I barely get what I'm saying myself. Bottom line is, ditching you was never an option."

Monika gave Sara a thump on the shoulder and glanced outside the building. She could sense the snipers starting to congregate.

It was going to take more than just her to break through their ranks.

* * *

Then there was the abandoned property to the southwest of the West-port Building.

After surviving their clash with Barron, the first thing Sybilla and Erna did was head down a back alley so they could get treated. Neither of them had been wounded *too* badly, but they were covered in bumps and bruises.

The physician they were going to was one Klaus had found—a back-alley doctor who was willing to treat anyone as long as they had cash. According to Klaus's intel, they could also buy grenades and ammo there if the need arose. Major cities often had people like that who were willing to fill unique niches.

Supposedly, the doctor operated out of an abandoned eight-story multi-tenant building.

However, the only thing the two of them found in the secret fifth-floor clinic was the doctor's corpse. It had been hacked to pieces with a knife.

"There's someone here…," Erna said.

She was the first to notice what was up, and Sybilla grabbed her by the collar and took off at a run. They needed to get out of the building as soon as possible, but the hallway was already packed with people. There were ten of them, and they smiled with relief when they spotted Sybilla and Erna. There was no commonality between their gender or ages, but the one thing they did have in common was the fretful looks in their eyes.

Sybilla could tell—they were like Barron. They had been threatened into following the puppet master's orders.

"Tch."

She clicked her tongue and raced up the building's stairs. There was nowhere to run to up there, but it was the only direction she could go. She already knew there weren't any nearby buildings they could jump to.

This eight-story building was no different from a set of gallows.

"Yeep," Erna murmured uneasily.

"Don't you worry," Sybilla said as she pulled her along. "There ain't a snowball's chance in hell I'm lettin' someone who called me their big sister die."

Her words were confident, but it was an empty show of courage.

Defeating Barron had been grueling, and he was just one person.

Even if she and Erna both gave it their all, they had no real chance of beating a group of ten if everyone in it was as skilled as he had been.

It pained her to admit it, but there was only one way out of this.

They needed Klaus to come. He was the sole person who could save them.

On their own, all they could do was buy time.

A little bit before their teammates found themselves in peril, Lily and Annette were in an alleyway right beside the Westport Building.

"……………"

"……………"

The two of them lay prone on a roof and surveyed the scene down below. The cops had declared them fugitives and were running around searching for them. They must have also called for backup, as another five police cars had shown up, and the officers were scouring the area. The cops kept in touch with one another via walkie-talkies as they rushed from building to building.

Annette began rummaging around in her skirt like she'd just thought of something, then pulled out a large device. She extended its antenna and put its earpiece in her ear.

Lily did the same with the other earpiece.

The device was an intercept for the cops' radios. She could hear them angrily shouting.

"*Dammit, she got away! How could we let the killer escape like that?!*" "*This smells like organized crime. She set up a bunch of bombs to distract us, too.*" "*She must have her sights set on that big economics conference...*" "*Lillian Hepburn might be some sort of international terrorist. We need to void her passport. We're going to arrest that lowlife if it takes every officer in Mitario to do it!*"

Their voices were filled with fervor.

Annette took out her earpiece and grinned. "Looks like we're safe for now, yo."

Lily cradled her head in her hands. "Maybe, but now I have a rap sheet a mile long!"

An hour had passed since she nearly got arrested out by the hamburger shop. Annette had saved her right before the cops could cart her off to the station, and the two of them had fled. Then they'd set off bombs at various spots throughout the city and used the panicking crowds as cover before eventually arriving at the building they were at now.

"Wait, am I gonna get put on the Most Wanted list? How am I supposed to get home after the mission is over?"

"Hey, it's better than getting arrested."

"No, it isn't! I'd rather get arrested a hundred times over!"

Still, the fact remained that the immediate danger was behind them.

"Okay, so there was a *bit* of a kerfuffle," her savior Annette commented. Lily's first instinct was to offer a retort or two, but she realized that she ought to be thanking her.

"Our enemies must be behind this," Lily said with a big sigh. "I guess they have an insider at the station—someone important enough to be able to get those false charges to stick. They must have set me up once they realized how suspiciously I was acting."

"Should we kill them?"

"We can't. Even if we wanted to, we don't know who they are."

"We could just kill all the cops."

"Oh, Annette." Lily laughed. "You know, there aren't a lot of duos where *I* have to play the straight man."

In any case, it looked like the best course of action would be to let the police pass by, then have the Intel squad figure out what to do next. There weren't any pressing threats, so all they had to do was wait out the cops.

Lily knew her waitress uniform was a bit too conspicuous, so she began changing into the comfortable mission garb that Annette had brought for her. Putting it on always helped her get her head in the game.

Fortunately, they were on top of a building. There was no one else around.

However, Annette leaped at her the moment she started to pull down her skirt. "There's someone watching, Sis."

Lily's face went bright red. "A-a voyeur, you mean?"

"They're watching through a scope."

"Th-that's a pretty darn dedicated voyeur!"

"And they've got a rifle, too."

"Hey, that's no voyeur!"

A bullet whizzed over their heads as they threw themselves prone on the roof. Chunks of concrete went flying.

Thanks to the bullet hole's angle, they could tell that the sniper was shooting at them from a room in the Westport Building. Lily stayed hidden as she finished changing, then took stock of the situation.

The sniper's up on the thirty-ninth floor...and the Westport Building's the tallest place around, which means they can shoot whoever they want from up there.

She and Annette were using the edge of the roof for cover, but they'd be sitting ducks the moment they took even a step away from it. She hadn't heard a gunshot, so their foe must have been using a silencer or something. The police officers down below hadn't even noticed the sniper's presence.

Their assailant wasn't part of the police force, but they had clearly been in touch with them. Perhaps the same puppet master was pulling both of their strings.

Lily reached for Annette's radio interceptor. She could hear another set of voices mixed in with the cops' radio chatter.

"They're in that building over there. It's go time." "Ten-four." "Anything to avoid the pain." "Let's kill them." "Yes, let's." "If we don't kill them, we'll be punished."

Their Westport Building opponent wasn't working alone. A number of somber-sounding voices spoke up one after another.

By the sound of it, there were more than ten of them. And with the sniper pinning her and Annette down, they couldn't even flee.

In all her life, Lily had never felt more cornered than she did right then.

"......................................"

She was scared.

It was plain to see that the two of them weren't going to be able to get out of this alone. They were going to die. They were going to perish. They were going to push up daisies. Their lives were going to end, and there was nothing they could do about it.

The cold hard reality of the situation was that these weren't the kind of people who a pair of academy washouts could hope to defeat.

Lily clapped herself on the cheeks to kick her faltering heart back into gear.

Don't you give up, Lily. Make the impossible possible.

She closed her eyes, and Klaus's words echoed back through her mind.

"I'm appointing you Lamplight team leader," he'd said.

She knew that he'd done so only as a ploy to motivate her. If it weren't for that, he never would have assigned someone as clumsy and bereft of spy skills as her to the role. Looking at the situation objectively, there were far better people he could have chosen.

But that lie was precisely what let her hold her head high.

"Hey, Annette?"

"That's me!"

"Stop me if I'm talking nonsense here, but are you, like, secretly competent as heck?"

".........." Annette's eyes widened a little.

Not much could earn that sort of reaction out of her.

"I'm curious," she replied. "What makes you think that?"

"C'mon, give me *some* credit." Lily grinned. "I might not look like much, but I'm still the team leader. I just get this feeling from you that you've got all sorts of mad skills."

"........."

"I'll act as a decoy and draw them away. Once you're out, you need to report in to Intel ASAP. The others might be in trouble, too."

Given Annette's skills, Lily was confident she'd be able to give their enemies the slip and find her way to a nearby pay phone.

They needed to let the Intel squad know what was going on.

That way, their teammates' odds of surviving would rise dramatically, and the Intel squad could come up with a plan and get in touch with Klaus. It was the only countertactic available to them.

"I figure you know this already…" Annette's usual smile was gone. Her face was a mask devoid of emotion. "But they're gonna kill you, Sis."

"I'd like to see them try. I've got poison gas, poison foam, poison smoke screens… I'm a master when it comes to buying time."

"That stuff's useless. Has any of it ever worked on Klaus?"

Sometimes the truth was harsh.

Lily's poison didn't exactly have the best track record in her battles against elite spies. There was that one time she'd made a poison foam barricade and stopped White Spider in his tracks, but that was all.

Poison immunity was a powerful ability, make no mistake, but Lily hadn't exactly been using it to great effect.

Lily wound her pinkie around Annette's.

"Then, when we get back to Din, you should build me the best weapon ever. Something strong enough to take down Teach."

"........"

"Make me a spy gadget that'll blow my socks off, okay?"

".............."

This time, there was nothing little about how wide Annette's eyes went.

Lily had no idea what was going through her teammate's mind. She had never really understood Annette. However, she looked her square in the eyes all the same.

Eventually, Annette squeezed Lily's pinkie back with hers.

Her trademark innocent smile returned to her face.

"You got it, yo. With my tinkering and your poison, I'll be able to whip up something *real* nasty."

"Heh. Teach won't know what hit him."

They let go of each other's pinkies at the same time.

Lily held her gun at the ready and began relocating. Doing so made her a juicy target for the sniper, and she was going to have to rely on instinct alone to dodge the bullets until she made it inside the building.

One wrong move, and her life would end.

"All right, here I go," Annette said, smiling sweetly as Lily rushed into mortal peril. "Time to leave Lily to die!"

It was a cruel, heartless option to take.

However, it was the best one they had available.

As Lily drew the sniper's attention, Annette got to work relocating as well. She leaped across to the next building over so she could escape the siege.

Now it was Lily's job to distract their foes until Annette was free and clear.

I gotta fool them all so Annette can get to that pay phone and report in to Intel!

As she dodged the first sniper shot by the skin of her teeth, she bit down on her lip.

As Lamplight's leader, the time had come for her to put her life on the line.

It was there, alone and imperiled, that her worth as a spy was going to be tested.

The distress beacons kept flashing.

Their teammates were in danger in three places at once, and none of them was strong enough to make it out on their own.

Thanks to Lily's noble sacrifice, the Intel squad had a full rundown of the situation.

Now it was up to them to figure out a plan that could turn their desperate position around.

However, none of that knowledge did Thea a lick of good. All she could do was clutch the receiver and stare off into space.

Who... Who are these people?!

She cradled her head in her hands and began hyperventilating.

She didn't know if Purple Ant was the one pulling the strings, but whoever it was, they were killing anyone even vaguely suspicious who showed up around the conference. This wasn't the kind of battle she and the others were equipped to fight. There were no tactics or schemes for them to see through, just sheer, overwhelming numbers. If you wanted to kill a spy, that was one of the surest ways to do it.

"What...can we do...?"

She was the commander. She knew she needed to come up with a plan, but she could hardly even think straight.

Tears began welling up in her eyes, and they refused to stop. She knew that her teammates might be dying that very moment, and the mental image of their corpses crowded out every other thought in her brain.

Over on the other side of the room, Grete hurried into her bedroom.

"Grete?"

Thea hurriedly followed after her.

Grete stripped off her clothes and began donning a man's suit.

"I'll disguise myself as the boss...," she said, her voice calm and collected. "If our opponents are working for the Empire, then they should know what the boss looks like. Seeing me will shake them. From there, Monika and I can work together to escape the danger."

In other words, she was planning on heading into the fray.

It was a brave thing to do, especially for someone as poor at fighting as she was.

However, she and Monika had both received Klaus's seal of approval. Together, they stood a decent chance of successfully escaping, and with Sara there, too, their odds of surviving weren't half bad.

"What do we do about Lily's and Sybilla's spots, then?" Thea asked.

"...The boss is around, and with how big a commotion this is, I find it hard to imagine he wouldn't notice what's going on. I'm sure he'll rush over to help," Grete coolly concluded as she finished putting on her disguise. She was the spitting image of Klaus. The mere sight of him sent relief flooding through Thea—

"W-wait, hold on!"

—but there was one concern she just couldn't shake.

"The numbers don't add up!" she said. She could feel a pain burning in her chest.

"........."

"There are three places that need backup. If you go to one and Teach goes to another, what do we do about the last one?"

"Thea..." Grete's expression hardened. She squeezed her fists tight. "We have to do the best we can with what we have..."

"___!"

Thea picked up what Grete was putting down.

She knew full well that they couldn't save everyone. They were too short on resources. Lamplight simply didn't have three people strong enough to deal with the three crises, so looking at the situation rationally, it was the only logical conclusion.

Even so, Grete steeled herself and headed for the door. She was going to save everyone she could.

"How do you do it?!" Thea cried pathetically. "How can you be so brave?"

"What do you mean...?"

"Please, I don't understand! What do I do? I don't have the kind of ingenuity you do, and I don't have the mental fortitude to dive into danger like that. What can someone who gets crushed by her failures even do?"

She needed Grete to guide her.

She needed Grete to show her what to do, just like she'd been doing all mission long.

"I'm not strong at all…," Grete said, shaking her head. "All I have is a desire to repay the boss. You might call it dependence or perhaps even an obsession. I want to do right by the man who returned my affection, even after my love was unrequited."

Unrequited? Something must have happened there.

However, Thea chose not to press her for details. She could tell by the passion in Grete's voice that it was a subject best not broached lightly.

The question was, how *did* Grete feel about Klaus? What was the nature of that affection that had surpassed even love? What could have been powerful enough to turn an academy washout into a brilliant spy?

"Thea," Grete ultimately said. "Please read back through the reports and figure out the best course of action you can take. I believe in you…"

That was all she had for her.

With that, Grete ran off, and Thea was left alone in the room. She could hear every police siren that roared past the apartment complex with alarming clarity. Her knees went weak, and she sank to the floor. Fat tears began rolling down her face and tumbling onto her hands. The tears were fearfully hot.

Now she realized just how truly powerless she was.

There's nothing I can do…

Could she rush over and help her allies? Maybe, but a fat lot of good it would do.

Her ability wasn't suited for combat.

She had a power called "negotiation," but it came with a prerequisite. To use it, she needed to first lock eyes with her target for several seconds. That made it useless against anyone who was actively trying to kill her. Even if she made it to one of the fights successfully, all she would do was slow the others down.

She was helpless to save her team.

In fact, she was helpless to do anything but sit on the floor of her apartment.

I'm a joke of a spy and a failure as a commander...

In the end, she'd delegated everything to Grete. Grete had called the shots, and Thea had done nothing but nod along. It was pathetic, was what it was. And now that Grete was gone, all she was doing was sitting on the floor and crying.

"Ms. Hearth..." She whispered her idol's name. "What can I do? What is it you even saw in me...?"

Seven years ago, she had met a mighty spy.

Not only did the woman save her, she gave her life purpose, too.

"You'll be the strongest spy around."

"But the thing is: I don't want you to become just any old spy. I want you to become a hero and save your enemies, too."

Hearing her say that had filled Thea with joy. She dreamed of a bright future, one where she joined Inferno someday and worked side by side with Hearth.

But reality had different plans.

Inferno got destroyed before she had a chance to join it.

Hearth had died after getting betrayed by an ally.

And Thea's dreams of becoming a hero who could save her enemies had led to her enemies manipulating her and laughing in her face.

Matilda's mockery had been a bucket of cold water for her.

Now, on top of that, her teammates were improving without her, she had failed in her duty as their commander, and she was doing nothing while their lives were in jeopardy.

"I wish I could just disappear..."

She dug her nails into the floor and wailed.

"What is someone as useless as me doing here anyway?!"

She pounded the floor again and again.

"I wish I could just disappear!" she shouted. "I'm too soft on myself, I'm too soft on my enemies, I don't have any real talents, I let myself feel superior to the others just because I have a little bit of sexual experience, I leave everything up to my teammates, and I act full of myself when I'm not even the team leader! I'm the weakest, most childish girl on the team, and I wish I could just die!"

"Hey, Sis."

Suddenly, a voice came through the receiver.

She hadn't realized it, but her call with Annette was still connected.

"*I don't want you to disappear, yo.*"

"Annette…"

"*I had fun last month. You know, when you did all that stuff for me,*" Annette went on in the kind of tone you would use to comfort a child.

It made it hard to tell which of them was really the older of the two.

"*I was surprised. I was all, She's such a meddler, and she never actually accomplishes anything, and all she's good for is being a slut.*"

"You, uh, have a way with words…"

Thea hadn't known that about her.

"*But it's not like I hate you or anything.*" Annette went on. "*Yo, Flower Garden asked me to do something. She said there was some info she wanted to pass along to you.*"

"She did?"

"*According to her investigation, there's this rumor going around the city. Something about a hero who rushes over to save people who are in the depths of despair.*"

"A hero…?"

The word reminded Thea of something, and she quickly remembered what that was. "Monika said something similar in her report. She said that Purple Ant's minions believe in some sort of hero."

That coed named Miranda had told them as much after her suicide attempt.

"*I wonder if the hero will come for me?*" she'd said.

Come to think of it, Sybilla had mentioned the same thing. Right before Barron passed out, he had muttered something about a hero as well. Thea hadn't given it much thought, but with all those data points in tandem, it didn't feel like it was just an idle rumor anymore. It was like someone was spreading it on purpose.

"But what does it mean? Did someone working with Purple Ant start it…?"

"*Apparently, the rumor even includes what the hero looks like.*"

That little tidbit hadn't been in either of the reports. Lily must have done some digging.

When Thea pressed the receiver against her ear, Annette said something wholly unexpected.

* * *

"According to Flower Garden, people are saying that the hero is a beautiful girl with black hair."

"What?"

That was pretty darn specific. When most people heard the word *hero*, they tended to think of a large, muscular man. Who was spreading the rumor, and to what end? Thea had no clue.

But to make things even more peculiar...

"Wait, that's exactly what *I* look like!"

The description matched Thea to a T. She had dark hair, she was a girl, and she was beautiful. Three for three.

"This next part is a message from Flower Garden."

Annette went on.

"'Pretty lucky, huh? Now, go piggyback off the rumor and become a hero for real.' That's what she wanted you to hear. Now I gotta get back to her."

After one-sidedly relaying the message, Annette hung up.

None of it made sense. Had Thea gotten lucky with the rumor's specifics, or was there more to it? Could a rumor that convenient really spread by mere happenstance?

"What... What does it all mean?"

She set down the receiver and moaned.

There was so much she didn't understand, but at least she'd managed to collect herself. Crying wasn't going to accomplish anything. Her team needed her, and she was going to do whatever little she could to help.

She stared intently at the wall.

Klaus's apartment was just on the other side, and he'd given them a copy of his key. Grete had used it to sneak in on numerous occasions, though she'd gotten thrown out each time.

Right now, there was a man being held prisoner in there.

Thea wasn't strong enough to save her friends. But she knew someone who was.

She took a deep breath.

This is all I can do for them.

Thea followed Grete's instructions and read back over the reports before heading next door.

The lights were off, and the apartment was dark. Klaus wasn't there, of course. He was off on the front lines, doubtless fighting fierce battles of his own against Purple Ant's minions.

The living room was neat and tidy, and it had none of the characteristic smells to it that domestic life usually carried. Beside it, one of the doors was locked up tight.

Thea used her key, gingerly opened the door, and found a gaunt man sitting on a chair within. His arms were tied up behind him and bound with heavy chains. It was like his captor had been afraid of what might happen if the man was allowed to move so much as a single finger.

"I figured it was about time."

It was Roland—the Imperial assassin she and Klaus had captured.

Despite his body being bound from head to toe, his eyes still gleamed with a fiery light, and he was just as inscrutably intimidating as ever. It might have just been Thea's imagination, but he seemed even more intense than he had before. His prolonged captivity had caused him to grow weaker and thinner and closer to death, all of which served to make his presence that much more striking.

His smug grin told Thea everything she needed to know.

This was his plan all along. He knew it would come to this!

He knew about Purple Ant. He knew about Purple Ant's ability and methods. He knew that the city was completely under Purple Ant's control. And he knew that Lamplight didn't have the combat assets to stand up to him.

Roland let out a shrill laugh. "What's the matter? Cat got your tongue?" he said in an overfamiliar tone. "Come on. This is, what, the fourth time we've met? You gotta stop being so afraid of me, kid."

However, Thea still couldn't get the words out. Roland had nearly killed her on two separate occasions. Even with him restrained, her fear refused to subside. It took everything she had just to keep her knees from rattling.

Roland stared at her mockingly, then laughed. "Heh. Looks like everything's going right according to plan. Purple Ant's Worker Ants are destroying you people. But hey, it's not your fault. There's no way you could take 'em down without advance warning. And see, that's how I know what you came to me for."

"........."

"You want me to save your teammates, right?"

She did.

Roland was the only one who could do it. He might not have been on Klaus's level, but his assassination skills were still best in class. There were crises in three different locations, and saving everyone was going to require more manpower. At the rate things were going, Lamplight was going to suffer casualties.

Thea clenched her fists.

The thing was, how could she trust him?

A look of sympathy crossed Roland's eyes. "Sure, I'll do it." He gave her a friendly smile. "What can I say? I've grown a soft spot for you guys. I'll lend you a hand."

"........."

"Hey, don't look so surprised. I'm being serious here. So come on—let me free."

Thea could feel her heart tighten, like someone had just grabbed it and was squeezing down. This was the moment. Her teammates were in peril, and she had one decisive choice to make.

She could release Roland, or she could ignore him.

There was nobody around she could ask for advice. Grete was gone, as was Klaus. This was a choice she was going to have to make on her own.

Roland clicked his tongue. "What's the holdup? If you keep dawdling, people are gonna die."

".................."

"You really want to let your teammates get killed 'cause you couldn't make up your mind?"

Thea remained silent as she tried to use her unique talent.

Once she locked eyes with someone, she could suss out their deepest desires. All she needed to do was fulfill that condition, and her ability would tell her what Roland really wanted. Then she could use that to get him under her thumb.

If I could just look him in the eye...!

She had made countless attempts to do just that. It was an easy enough feat to pull off on men allured by her beauty, but each time she tried it on Roland, he quickly averted his gaze.

"All right, what's going on here?" Roland sighed. "You get off on looking me in the eye or something? Look, we both know that's not what's up. Here's a pro tip: If you're too scared to even talk to someone, trying to look 'em in the eye over and over is just gonna make 'em suspicious."

"........."

"Your little party trick's not gonna work on me, kid."

He was stonewalling her. It was just like with Klaus—his spy's intuition was telling him to be on alert. Thea had never succeeded in using her ability on an elite spy. It hadn't worked on Matilda, either.

She was out of options. She had been able to pull it off against Monika by kissing her, but getting that close to Roland would be too dangerous to even try. The moment she laid her lips on his, he could easily rip her tongue out.

There's nothing... Nothing I can do...

Time was slipping away.

She couldn't bring herself to risk it all by untying him. If she did, she'd be doing the exact same thing she did last time. It would be just like how she had followed Matilda's lead and rescued her without ever managing to find out who she really was.

The laughter still echoed in her ears.

"Thea, honey, you're a nobody."

She couldn't make that same mistake again.

Suddenly, Roland spoke up. "...Oh, I get it. Not too long ago, you blew it."

This time, his voice wasn't menacing at all. It was gentle.

"I can see it all over your face. I shouldn't have been such a dick to you. Sorry about that. I'm a little on edge myself."

He shook his head slightly.

He's apologizing? An elite assassin *is apologizing to* me?

As Thea stood dumbfounded, Roland made an embarrassed gesture with his chin. "I guess that makes two of us. I blew it pretty badly, too."

At long last, Thea finally managed to speak. It was only two words, but still. "You did?"

"You were there, weren't you? You saw me take on Bonfire and get my ass handed to me on a silver platter. And after all that embarrassing shit I spouted off about being his rival or whatever, too."

"Ah, right..."

"You mind if I tell you a little story about myself? Don't worry—it won't take long."

He gave her a thin smile.

Not even the Foreign Intelligence Office had been able to turn up anything on Roland's background. She couldn't help but lend an ear.

"I used to be a pretty boring dude. I was born to a couple of well-to-do parents here in Mouzaia, and they told me I needed to inherit the family business. So that's what I spent my life getting ready to do—right up until I met a weirdo named Purple Ant and his posse."

"Purple Ant…"

"Apparently, he took one look at me and saw I had potential, so he kidnapped me and molded me into a spy. Honestly, I didn't end up minding it that much. I was good at this stuff. I mean *good*. I surpassed the other Worker Ants in a flash and got all sorts of special treatment. Then I went around the world, killing whichever spies and politicians he told me to."

Roland shrugged.

"But in the end…it got boring."

"………"

"You get it, right? There was no *goal* behind the killings I did. All I was doing was following his orders. But he'd brainwashed me, so I couldn't disobey them. I was a slave. A puppet. A machine. The conveyer belt brought me people, and I slapped a big old 'assassinated' sticker on them. There was nothing more to it."

Thea couldn't begin to comprehend Roland. He was talking about ending human lives like it was some sort of menial labor.

However, she felt like she understood him a bit better now.

Killing people was too easy for him. Due to his profound talent, assassination had been reduced to a mere item on his daily itinerary. Most people didn't give cracking eggs or shopping for groceries a second thought, and for him, crushing human hearts was the same way.

"The question I asked myself was, what was my purpose in life? I spent ages trying to puzzle it out."

"I see…"

"But a couple of years later, I ran into someone who told me something. *'I know someone who can fill that void in your heart,'* they said. It felt like I'd just heard a prophecy. Apparently, there was this monster who was stronger than anyone, who no one could kill, and who could complete any mission. I figured that meeting him would give my life meaning." Roland laughed, like it was all one big joke. "But you saw how well that turned out for me. I couldn't even lay a finger on the guy."

"........."

"See? We're not so different, you and I. We both made a big blunder that broke our hearts into pieces, and neither of us has any idea how we're supposed to get our lives back on track. You feel me?"

He had seen right through her.

She could picture herself tied up right where Roland was now. Maybe they were the same. Her body may have been unfettered, but her heart was bound up just as tight as he was. Neither of them had been able to recover from their crippling failure. Not Thea, not Roland.

"Come on—let's you and me team up. We'll be fellow failures, trying to take our lives back together."

His voice was reassuring. So much so that Thea had to quickly grab hold of her wavering heart.

"What you're proposing doesn't make sense," she said, her voice so feeble, she barely even sounded like herself. "Going off what you just told me, you work for Purple Ant."

"Yup. He calls his minions his 'Worker Ants,' and I'm one of them."

"But if that's the case, you shouldn't be able to betray him. The reports I got said that his hold over his minions was absolute."

"Hey, don't lump me in with those losers. He doesn't have as much sway over me."

"What proof do you have of that?"

"I'm still here, aren't I? Haven't you heard? All the other Worker Ants try to kill themselves when they're beaten."

He had a point.

According to Monika's and Sybilla's reports, their defeated foes had made attempts on their own lives and avoided treating their own wounds the moment they were defeated. But not Roland. His story checked out.

"Now it's time to make a choice. Are you gonna let me out or aren't you?"

He quietly gave her a look.

She was out of time. The more she hesitated, the more the opportunity slipped away.

Visions of her teammates flickered through her mind.

They had spent so many happy days together living and laughing under the same roof.

Whenever Thea's stories started to get sexual, Lily would always run away in embarrassment. Sybilla would feign exasperation but secretly be interested. Sara would turn bright red. Beside her, Grete would diligently take notes, and Monika would give her an icy look as she covered up Erna's ears. Annette would cock her head quizzically, but she always seemed to be enjoying herself.

Occasionally, Klaus would stop by as they were partying it up in the dining room. When he did, the team would hound him with questions about his romantic history, and he would grimace at them and flee. Lily would try to stop him, but she'd invariably end up tripping, causing laughter to fill the dining room.

Thea wanted to make sure they could go back to those halcyon days. She wanted to complete the mission so they could spend their time together in blissful harmony. And she didn't care what she had to give up to do it.

She unfastened Roland's restraints.

Using her spare key, she removed the chains tying him up. All in all, there had been more than twenty locks holding them together.

The moment the last lock came open, Roland slumped forward, and his face slammed hard into the floor. He had been tied up for so long that his muscles weren't working right.

A surge of worry coursed through Thea. Was he really going to be able to defeat their foes in that state?

After lying on the ground for a good long while, he grabbed the chair and began hoisting himself up. Even after he successfully rose to his feet, his torso continued swaying every which way, and his head wobbled back and forth.

Thea rushed over to help support him. That was when she got her first good look at his face.

Roland grinned.

"One more thing, for the record."

He gave his body a big stretch.

"That thing about me being special was true. The order Purple Ant gave me for what to do if I lost wasn't to kill myself. It was to trick my enemies and make my way back by any means necessary."

A horrible creaking sound rang out from every joint in his body—so loud it was like his bones were cracking. As it did, his muscles settled back into place. His torso, so wobbly just moments before, snapped to a stop as he stood there, imposing and dignified.

Now she'd really gone and done it.

She'd freed an assassin feared the world over.

Thea inched away. As her back bumped against the bedroom's window, Roland closed the distance between them in the blink of an eye. He was in full form again, and he grabbed Thea by the throat and pressed her hard against the wall without giving her a moment to flee.

The latch behind her popped free, and the window swung open.

Thea's torso protruded out the opening eight stories off the ground.

"You're not the brightest, are you, kid? I can't believe you fell for it that easy," Roland sneered as he squeezed down on her neck.

The king's rule spread despair all throughout Mitario.

What could they possibly do to prevail?

When Thea woke up, she found herself lying on a cold floor.

She was somewhere underground. The room had no windows, and its indirect lighting only dimly illuminated her surroundings. Still, she could tell that she was in a small bar, one with only two seats. One of the walls was lined with rows of spirits, and there was a slender man polishing a glass behind the counter.

Upon touching the floor, Thea realized that something was odd about it. She squinted at it. The entire floor was red with blood. Her gut told her that no one person had that much blood in them. Several people must have been killed there.

"Where…am I?" she asked, but the bartender said nothing.

Her gun was gone, but she wasn't bound.

When she sat up, she heard footsteps coming from behind the door beside the counter.

Then a man came in wearing a hat and a suit. He had a kind look about him, and his smiling eyes in particular gave him a gentle impression. He seemed like the sort of person children just adored.

When he spotted Thea, he nodded slightly. "Escaping on his own and capturing his foe to boot? He never fails to impress. That's some frightening talent he has."

Thea knew exactly who he was.

He might have looked harmless, but in truth, he was the lowest of the low.

"Are you Purple Ant?"

"I see I can skip the introduction." He tipped his hat and smiled. "It's so nice to meet you. I am sorry, though. I'm a bit short on time, so I'm afraid I have to skip straight to killing you. As you die, do be sure to leave behind your dying words. I would love to hear what you have to say."

"How...thoughtful."

"Oh, indeed. I make it a habit to be kind to women."

"Somehow, I find that difficult to believe."

"I'll have you know that while I may not look it, I'm actually quite the gentleman. I always feel remorse when I hit a woman."

Thea was well past caring about the man's messed-up moral code.

However, she had a pretty good idea of why he was in such a hurry.

"I presume you're going after Teach?"

"That I am. I'm hoping that showing him your corpse will throw him for a bit of a loop. He's a tenacious one; I'll give him that. I sent seventy-three Worker Ants after him, and they still haven't put him down. It makes a man wonder, is that boy really human?"

Just as she assumed, Klaus was locked in battle. By the sound of it, he was surrounded by waves of enemies and was unable to move about freely.

The bartender offered Purple Ant a gun, and Purple Ant took the Mouzaia-made revolver and began diligently loading it one shot at a time. He almost seemed to be musing over which bullet to kill her with.

Thea bit her lip. It was all too obvious what was about to happen.

*　*　*

She was going to die, and Lamplight was going to lose to Purple Ant. The numbers he had at his disposal were beyond anything they'd imagined. Not only was he going to use those numbers to trample them into the ground, Klaus was going to be so busy with the seventy-plus Worker Ants that he wouldn't make it in time to save any of the others.

If everything was as it seemed, that was how it would all play out.

Thea shook her head.

"You really are unbeatable."

"Hmm?"

"I can say with full confidence that as of this moment, you're the strongest spy in the city. It hardly seems fair. Picking a fight with you now was the worst move we could have made."

"Well, yes. I'm the king," Purple Ant replied offhandedly. "Did you only just realize that?"

He was an uncommonly confident man, but perhaps that was to be expected. It was only natural that one would feel omnipotent with power such as his. His ability let him control people through pain and command them so completely, he could even order them to kill themselves.

With his slaves filling the streets of Mitario the way they did, he truly was this city's king.

It seemed foolish to even think of opposing him.

"But that's just it. *As of this moment*, you're unbeatable, and picking a fight with you *now* was the worst move we could have made."

The tactics they'd been using had been fundamentally misguided. If they wanted to take him down, doing so now would be pointless. Tons of spies had tried to do just that, and tons of spies had failed.

They needed to change the way they approached it.

Now, Thea finally understood how to break free from the despair he'd created.

"If we want to win, we need to look at it all differently."

She went on.

"We can't beat you *now*. We have to use *the passage of time* to take you down."

She had found the answer. The intel her teammates had risked their lives to gather had led her to the truth.

The moment she worked it out, all the little things that had seemed off finally made sense. Now she understood how Purple Ant had reacted to them so quickly, as well as what the true meaning behind the rumor spreading throughout Mitario was.

There was only one way to overcome despair—*and it was to guess the name of the woman who'd died there.*

And so she posed a question to Purple Ant.

"Let me ask you this: *Six months ago*…did you kill Ms. Hearth here?"

Interlude

Purple Ant ④

"Hearth," Purple Ant declared. "That's your code name, isn't it?"

"...That's right."

His captive—that was to say, Hearth—gave him a defeated nod.

Even though he was the one who'd made the guess, Purple Ant still found himself surprised.

His mission had been to annihilate any spy who came near the Tolfa Economic Conference so as to whittle away at their enemy nations. Even though the six-month-long conference had *only just begun*, he had already taken out boatloads of notorious agents.

On top of that, he had also captured a woman he suspected was a spy for the Din Republic. White Spider had warned him to be on guard against Bonfire, so he'd taken her to use as a hostage to lure him in, but he never imagined that she would end up being *the* Hearth.

Purple Ant took another look at the woman lying before him.

Now that he knew her code name, he was even more shocked at how young she seemed. No matter how you added it up, she had to at least be in her late thirties, but she certainly didn't look it. Her long hair was a fiery crimson, and her eyes—the right one of which had a deep gash under it—had an energy in them that bordered on ferocity.

Hearth pressed down on the bullet wound in her torso and smiled. "I have to say, I thought you'd have me pegged a lot earlier." She had already lost a lot of blood, enough so that it was forming a pool around her feet. Her skin was deathly pale.

Most people would have simply let themselves drift away.

"Well, would you look at that. You can talk just fine," Purple Ant replied. "Why the silence, then?"

"I was doing my best to buy whatever time I could. But it's too late for that now. Ah, what a shame. I guess this is where I die. There's no surviving an injury like this." The look on her face seemed almost refreshed. "I really am surprised it took you so long to find me out, though. All my information's been leaked, hasn't it?"

"That it has. And besides, you were famous to begin with."

"That's hardly something I'm proud of, given that I'm a spy and all. Why didn't you see through me from the start, then?"

Purple Ant hesitated a moment before answering.

It was rare beyond words for him to show anyone such consideration.

"Because of how weak you are."

"Oh dear."

"Looking at your long list of accomplishments, then looking at you, you're too frail to fit the profile."

There was no shortage of legends about her.

The information she gave the Allies about the Imperial Army during the Great War had been directly responsible for bringing the conflict to an end. The Empire cursed the very ground she walked on, but as a fellow agent, Purple Ant couldn't help but respect her.

"I never realized how rapidly your illness had progressed," he said. "Why, your judgment was so dulled and your body was so weak that it only took fifty of my Worker Ants to bring you down. How could you possibly be Hearth? I asked myself."

"Alas, you've got me there. Nowadays, I'm just a dried-out husk."

"You're at, what, a tenth the strength you had in your heyday?"

"Please, don't sell me short. I'm at least a *ninth* the woman I was."

He couldn't tell if that was her bragging or being modest.

She shook her head in self-deprecation. "Do you mind if I ask you a question of my own? You seem pretty concerned about Klaus, but is he even coming? I don't actually know, myself."

"I haven't the faintest, either. My teammates set a trap for him, but it sounds as though he escaped. At the moment, the Empire has no idea where he is. I had hoped that capturing you would be enough to get him to show his face, but..."

"But he hasn't even come to this nation, has he?"

"Unfortunately, that does seem to be the case."

Purple Ant glanced down at Hearth's flank. The pool of blood was getting bigger. She didn't have long left.

"It's a sorry way to go," he said. "Ravaged by disease, betrayed by a teammate, having the rest of your teammates killed, coming here to Mitario to fight all on your own, then getting overrun by my Worker Ants and breathing your last in a basement where no light can reach?"

"........."

"This is it, is it? This is how the woman revered as the Greatest Spy in the World dies?"

Sweat gushed from Hearth's brow as she smiled. "This is how all operatives meet their end."

"Ah, I see. I'll be sure to remember that."

Purple Ant was under no illusions that his own demise would be any more peaceful. Still, something about Hearth's impeding death filled him with a sense of emptiness.

It all felt so anticlimactic.

Even in the Empire, there were tons of people who respected her. The artistic ways she had of snatching up information were so magical that even her bested foes couldn't help but sigh in amazement. Serpent itself had a number of her admirers in its ranks.

"In short," he went on, "spies take nothing to their graves but despair."

"Oh, quite the contrary," she said, denying his statement flat-out. Even with death fast approaching, she smiled nonetheless. "Right now, I'm full to the brim with hope. Why, the future's so bright, it's hurting my eyes."

"All your teammates except Bonfire are dead. And sooner or later, Bonfire will die, too."

"No, he won't. Klaus is strong." Her voice rang with confidence. "He's... He's my beautiful boy, that's what he is. We might not be related by blood, but he's my son all the same, and he inherited every skill Inferno had to offer. In all my life, I've never met anyone as talented as he is."

"........."

"I promise, he can satisfy your desiccated heart. I swear it on my life."

"Desiccated? My heart isn't desiccated."

Purple Ant wasn't sure what to make of her promise, but he made sure to file it away in his brain anyway.

It was clear just from listening to her that the things she said had the power to etch themselves deep in people's hearts. Sometimes, words were more than just words.

"And he's not the only one," she continued. "There's another child who inherited my will as well."

"Oh?"

That was news to him.

As far as they knew, Hearth didn't have any blood relatives, nor was she close with anyone outside of Inferno. And she certainly didn't have an apprentice.

"I saw it in her eyes. She inherited my will, and someday, she's going to make my dream come true. She'll save more people than a dried-out husk like me could ever hope to."

"And who exactly is she, this mystery child of yours?"

"Oh, I couldn't say... It's been seven years since the last time I saw her. I'd love to see what kind of person she's grown into since then."

Hearth shook her head. The look on her face was so serene, it was hard to believe she was at death's door.

Purple Ant squinted at her. "I'm finding this all a little difficult to believe."

There was a good chance Hearth was using her final moments to spread misinformation in an attempt to shake him up. There was no way she was actually placing all her hopes on some child she hadn't seen in seven years.

However, her claim reminded him of something.

That word *save* had been showing up in the odd rumor circulating around Mitario, too.

"Wait, was it you?" he asked. "Are you the one who's been feeding my Worker Ants those weird rumors?"

"Oh my, whatever might you be talking about?"

"The stuff about a dark-haired hero coming to people who are in the depths of despair."

Originally, he'd written it off as meaningless nonsense. He never would have imagined that the one and only Hearth was the culprit behind it. Still, even with her back totally against the wall, spreading rumors like that would have been child's play for her.

"You found me out, huh?" She sighed. "I mean, how could I not feel bad for them? Those…'Worker Ants,' you called them? Your minions needed the light of hope. So I planted it deep in their brains for them."

"Spreading false hope? You're crueler than you look." Purple Ant scoffed. "And besides, they don't deserve your sympathy. The people I dominate are a bunch of human scum who make their livings off the misfortune of others. Losing the war drove the Empire to destitution, and these people are growing fat and rich off our losses. I mean, did you even *see* how gaudy that Main Street of theirs is?"

He thought back to the rows of skyscrapers and glowing neon billboards.

All that wealth had come from selling goods to the countries suffering on the Great War's front lines. The resources they'd supplied the Allies with had played a huge role in the Imperial Army's downfall.

"After the wounds we suffered in the Great War, we have every right to hate these people."

Purple Ant had no pity to spare for the people he forced to give up their lives and become Worker Ants. Compared to the way the Empire's people were suffering under the massive war reparations, they were getting off easy.

If anything, they should be grateful they got to live under the rule of a king as benevolent as him.

Hearth gave him an icy look. "You sicken me. You and your whole rotten ideology. I don't know where you get off playing the victim, but I still remember full well the lives we lost when you people invaded the Republic," she said pointedly. "See, a hero doesn't leave anyone behind."

"…What?"

"Do you know what your weakness is? Your domination can't control people's hearts. No matter how much violence you threaten them with and how much despair you plunge them into, you can never extinguish their light." She went on confidently, her voice proud and dignified. "The hope I gave them wasn't false. A hero *is* coming. She'll come to Mitario. Klaus will bring her. She'll see the light dwelling in their hearts, and as your natural predator, she'll save this city's people."

Hearth let go of her wound, reached into her pocket, and withdrew a bullet from within. She must've kept spares. She held it between her fingers and showed it to Purple Ant.

"She's my final bullet, the one I put everything into—and she's going to tear through you."

Now she was really talking nonsense. Her judgment must truly be shot.

"Please stop ruining my image of you," Purple Ant said. "I derive no pleasure from seeing you like this. Oh, how far you've fallen. I guess the disease must have reached your brain."

He didn't even want to look at her anymore. At this point, putting her out of her misery would be a mercy.

He raised his revolver and pointed it at her forehead.

"Then I have one last thing to say." Hearth turned her gaze toward the entrance. Blood dripped off her hand as she reached out. "Klaus, help!"

"........."

Purple Ant whirled around on reflex. Had Bonfire really come?

However, there was no one there. The door was still closed. He looked back and found Hearth sticking out her tongue. "Did you fall for it?"

He pulled the trigger.

Hearth's body jerked as the bullet impaled her skull and penetrated her brain. Purple Ant fired another five shots. Each one of them hit an organ. The pool of blood grew bigger than ever and stained Purple Ant's shoes a deep red.

The bullet slipped from Hearth's fingers.

Purple Ant looked away from the corpse and, with a dazed look on his face, gave his pet dog a sharp kick. "I need you to deliver the corpse to the Din Republic. Make sure nobody can follow your trail back here."

Then he left the bar.

He felt no sense of accomplishment, just a gnawing emptiness. Even a spy as legendary as Hearth had still died just like anyone else.

He stared up at the Westport Building as it towered into the sky.

To him, its wordless silence made it look like a gravestone.

Chapter 5

Domination and Negotiation

"That's right, Hearth died in this very room. How did you know?"

The moment Purple Ant's reply reached her ears, Thea closed her eyes.

She saw no reason to answer his question. And even if she'd wanted to, she was too busy processing her feelings toward her savior.

Her chest throbbed. Hearth had died all alone in this basement. Purple Ant had tormented her, then ended her life. Thea doubted that he had shown her so much as a shred of mercy. He had probably taken his time torturing her before ultimately ending her life.

It hurt more than she could say.

Hearth had died only halfway to her goal, and there were so many things she'd left unfinished.

In the time before she perished, however, she succeeded in leaving a message. Even with her back against the wall, even when she was in desperate peril, she planted a seed in the Worker Ants' hearts.

"A hero is coming. She'll have dark hair, and she'll rescue you from despair."

Because Hearth had remembered. She remembered her meeting with Thea seven years prior, and she remembered how that young girl had shared her dream. And so she pinned all her hopes on Thea and entrusted her with the task of defeating Purple Ant.

Thank you, Ms. Hearth. Thank you for remembering me for all these years...

Thea's tears flowed freely, and they refused to stop. How many times was it now that Hearth had lifted her heart up and saved her?

...No, that isn't quite fair. Ms. Hearth isn't the only one who helped me get back on my feet this time.

If it weren't for her teammates, Thea never would have arrived at the truth.

When Grete left, she had told her to look back through the reports. Those reports had come in from their allies, and while Grete would have normally told her to read them earlier, the situation had been a bit too pressing for that.

The thing was, those reports weren't just sitreps. They had messages attached to them, too.

Monika and Sara's report had a little something extra written at the end of the letter.

"Postscript: I'm working my butt off out here, so I expect no less from you guys. I'm talking to you here, slut. Get your shit together. Right now, you get zero out of a hundred."

It was classic Monika—harsh and to the point.

Then there had been a section in Sara's handwriting.

"I made sure that Miss Glint didn't see me writing this, but she's really worried about you, Miss Dreamspeaker. And I am, too, of course."

Thea laughed when she read that. Sara had been doing her level best to make sure Monika's kindness came through properly.

Sybilla and Erna had included messages with their report, as well.

"P.S. To the pervy one in the Intel squad: C'mon, pull yourself together already. You made the chosen group, remember? I try not to bring it up much, but I'm still kinda sore over not getting picked."

"I know just how hard you've been working, Big Sis. You're too kind for your own good, but that's what makes your ideas so wonderful. ~~Sincerely, Erna~~ (scratch that, I shouldn't include my real name)"

As for Annette and Lily, they'd already conveyed their sentiments over the phone.

"I don't want you to disappear, yo."

"Now, go piggyback off the rumor and become a hero for real."

And in Grete's case, she had said it in person.

"Figure out the best course of action you can take. I believe in you..."

All of Thea's teammates were cheering her on.

When she realized that, it had filled her heart with warmth.

I'm sorry, everyone. I'm sorry I made you all worry about me. Thinking back now, of course you saw what I was going through. I guess that's what happens when you live under the same roof.

Had they gone so far as to plan this all out, she wondered? Had they met up beforehand and decided that if she hadn't gotten back on her feet by the time the mission started heating up, they would write messages to her in their reports?

Lily was the one who'd masterminded it, no doubt. Sometimes, she thought less like a spy and more like a normal schoolgirl.

That said, their concern was truly touching.

Lastly, it was Klaus who had told her how to proceed once she'd finally rallied.

"Ruthlessness may have served the team well in the past, but the day will come when that empathy of yours is exactly what we need."

It had taken her a while, but she finally understood what he meant.

She was fine just the way she was. Klaus understood her ideals, and he didn't think there was a single thing wrong with them. She should have just trusted him all along. She should have believed him and worn her softhearted nature like a badge of honor.

She wished he could see her now.

She might have been soft, and it might not have taken much to crush her spirits, but she was about to put this despair to rest.

Adversity was nothing to be afraid of.

"Here I am, Purple Ant." She opened her eyes. "The hero has arrived."

"Well, aren't we feeling cocksure?"

"Oh, I am," Thea replied. "It's time to settle this."

She looked at Purple Ant head-on. Now she finally understood. This battle was hers to fight. She was the hero, and it was her job to strike down the king.

Purple Ant took off his hat with visible displeasure, then combed back his hair and redonned it. "The girl with dark hair. I see. So this 'hero' was you?" He gave her an annoyed frown. "You know, my heart leaped when I first got the call about you. But in the end, you're just a naive little girl who doesn't understand the situation she's in."

"Oh, I understand it perfectly well. I've been captured."

"And now you're going to die." Purple Ant glanced over at the bartender, then snapped his fingers. "Perhaps a crueler method would be best. That would put a nice little bow on all this."

The man had been polishing glasses through their whole conversation, but now his whole body quivered. He looked to be in his late twenties, and up until Purple Ant called to him, he had been rooted firmly in one place without so much as twitching. It was clear to see how honed his body was.

His expression had been calm and level, but the moment Purple Ant glared at him, he immediately began shaking.

"Allow me to introduce you two," Purple Ant said. "My friend here used to be a renowned martial artist, and it took ten Worker Ants just to restrain him. Ever since my torture, he's been polishing his techniques even further. Now he can dismember an adult man in thirty seconds flat." He snapped his fingers again. "If you don't have her in pieces within ten seconds, there'll be punishment. **Now kill her.**"

The bartender stooped below the counter, then rose back up holding a large ax. Without even pausing to adjust his grip, he leaped over the counter and swung his ax down at Thea's skull.

His expression was filled with a berserk fear, and his entire face was sweating.

"Stop."

The bartender's ax froze mid-swing. It was like someone had frozen time itself.

Purple Ant's eyes went wide.

The order just now had come from Thea's mouth, and it had overwritten Purple Ant's domination.

Thea reached up and touched her throat. "You recognize this voice, don't you, Mr. Bartender? You were here in the basement, and you saw Ms. Hearth, too."

A groan escaped the man's throat. "Guh…"

That voice was something Thea had inherited from Hearth. It was a perfect imitation of her tone, intonation, rhythm, and pitch. Thea had

lost her own voice at a young age, and it was only by mimicking Hearth's that she got it back.

Thea stood before the man and gently stroked his cheek. Gazing into his eyes as he stood motionless like that was trivial.

With that, she dredged up his deepest desires.

She smiled. "You've been waiting for a long time, haven't you? Ever since this voice told you that a hero was coming, you've been holding out hope. He's been controlling you through fear, but all the while, you've been desperately seeking that light."

To him, Thea's voice was like a panacea.

The idea Hearth planted deep in his heart had spent the past six months gestating, and it was ready to bloom.

"It's okay now. You can let me save you. I'm the dark-haired hero, and I'm here to help."

Thea wrapped her arms around the man and pulled him into a soft hug.

She embraced her foe. She comforted her foe. She loved her foe.

She swaddled him in her arms, rubbed his back, and held him in her bosom. Then she whispered the words he wanted to hear more than anything.

"You don't have to kill anyone anymore."

The man went limp, then clung tightly to her waist and began sobbing like a baby. Thea patted his head. "It's okay," she told him. "It's okay now."

Peering into his heart had told her everything she needed to know.

She knew he once had a woman he loved. How he had dreamed of marrying her, and how he'd built up his savings from the prize money he won in underground martial arts matches. How the day before he planned on proposing to her, he got attacked by hoodlums and tortured by Purple Ant. And how, unable to go against his fear, he strangled his girlfriend with his own two hands and became a slave who did nothing but kill.

Thea took his sins and his regrets and the hellish mess his life had become—and she forgave him for all of it.

She heard a big sigh coming from Purple Ant's direction.

"Well, I'll be. You overwrote my order. I must say, I'm shocked." He frowned. "Have you really thought this through, though? He's a serial killer, you know. I may be the one who gave the order, but that doesn't change the fact that he's ended more than a dozen lives. Can you really be sure he's even worth saving?"

"Without a moment's doubt."

"Then there's something wrong with you."

She didn't care what he said. She was proud of the path she'd chosen.

No matter how many times she lost heart, no matter how many times she got hurt, she would always have the will she'd inherited from Hearth.

"Well, breaking my hold on one man won't do you much good." Purple Ant took the revolver he'd been loading and snapped its cylinder into place. "I guess I'll just have to kill you myself. As a gentleman, it pains me to harm a woman, but we do what we must."

"I'm not certain you know what that word *gentleman* means."

"No, it's true. I hate hitting women. It always gives me the most embarrassing boner."

The moment Purple Ant leveled his revolver at her, the bartender quickly rose up and positioned himself so that he was shielding her. He wanted to protect her.

Thea was moved by his gallantry, but she had no intention of using him as a sacrifice. "I'm sorry, but fighting is hardly my forte. So instead, let me say this." She looked over at the entrance. "Teach, help!"

Purple Ant smirked, and for some reason, his eyes lit up with scorn. It was like they were saying, *I'm not falling for that again.*

And yet, a response came.

"That's what I'm here for," the voice said reassuringly.

Purple Ant gawked in horror as he whirled around.

There, standing in the entrance, was Klaus. He didn't appear to be wounded, but his clothes were drenched in the blood of others. It was hard to imagine just how intense the fights he'd been through were.

Klaus nodded. "You know, it's odd. It feels like those words have been waiting to reach me for the longest time. And like it's a shame that they haven't been able to do so until now."

He stared forlornly at the bloodstain on the ground.

Klaus's appearance had given Purple Ant quite the scare. His gaze flitted back and forth between Klaus and Thea. "So you're the Klaus I've heard so much about. How did you find this place?"

"I see no reason to tell you that."

"What happened to the seventy-three Worker Ants I sent after you?"

"I beat them all. Why do you ask?"

" " .... " "

Purple Ant and Thea both lapsed into silence.

The man defied belief.

A single Worker Ant had been enough to give the girls a close fight, and being attacked by just over ten at once had put their lives in grave danger. And yet, Klaus had taken on seventy-three of them and emerged victorious without suffering so much as a scratch.

"I don't blame you for being surprised." Klaus crossed his arms in satisfaction. "Against the World's Strongest, though, they didn't stand a—"

Thea cut him off. "Teach…"

"Hmm?"

"…you're on such a different level that the impressiveness of the feat doesn't really register."

"Really? That's kind of a bummer."

"You crossed that threshold where it's so unbelievable, we end up having no choice but to assume your opponents were secretly weak or something."

"Well, that doesn't seem fair at all." Klaus looked strangely hurt, but that was simply the truth of the matter. The feat *was* impressive, of course, but them's the breaks. "Each and every one of them was a force to be reckoned with."

After pleading his futile case one last time, Klaus turned and faced Purple Ant.

There were four people in the basement: Purple Ant, Thea, Thea's new ally the bartender, and now Klaus. That was all. There were no windows or anywhere to escape out of.

The tables had been completely turned.

Now it was Purple Ant who found himself in a crisis. How was he supposed to fight back against Klaus's superhuman combat skills?

"I see, I see. You're even more of a headache to deal with than the rumors said." Purple Ant shrugged. "But don't think you've won just because you took out my rank and file. You forget you're dealing with this city's king."

He was about to pull something.

The moment he sensed that, Klaus decided to make the first move. In the space of less than a second, he whipped out a revolver and shot it straight at Purple Ant.

But Purple Ant's shout came faster.

"Protect me!"

The bartender had been covering Thea, but now his body sprang into action. He was moving not intentionally but on pure reflex. Doing so had been drilled into his brain.

Klaus's bullet slammed right into the bartender's clavicle.

"Kill them. And don't believe their bullshit. **Kill. Kill. Kill,"** Purple Ant shouted at the top of his lungs. He was trying to overwrite Thea's words right back.

Then he dashed toward the back of the bar, making sure to keep the bartender between him and Klaus all the while. He pressed his hand against what looked to be a solid wall and pushed right through it.

"He has a secret passageway!"

He'd prepared an escape route for if he found himself in the worst-case scenario. He was a resilient one, that Purple Ant.

The bartender thrashed about in a deranged frenzy, and Klaus pinned him still while Thea spoke to him again to calm him down. She hadn't fully dispelled Purple Ant's domination yet. The man struggled and screamed in agony.

If they wanted to save the Worker Ants once and for all, they were going to have to defeat Purple Ant.

Klaus put the bartender to sleep by slipping him a sedative.

"Come on," Thea called over to Klaus. "We need to go after him."

However, Klaus just stared quietly at the floor. He'd noticed something. He stooped down and reached his hand under the chair.

"These are the rounds the boss always used."

There was a small bullet resting in his palm.

Sure enough, this was where she had been killed. In her last moments, her one final keepsake had rolled across the floor and been forgotten.

Klaus squeezed the bullet tight. "Let's go, Thea. We have some avenging to do."

"I'm right there with you, Teach. It's time we settled this."

Purple Ant had escaped down the hidden passageway, but he knew full well that it wouldn't keep them off his trail for long. His aim had been to buy time so he could marshal his remaining Worker Ants for a final stand.

The battle for Mitario was entering its final stage.

Klaus and Thea dashed through the secret passageway and soon emerged aboveground.

They looked up and found a huge building towering overhead. It was the skyscraper they'd seen so much of over the past few weeks that they were starting to get sick of it—the Westport Building. Who would've thought that Purple Ant's hideout would be smack-dab in the heart of the city?

Klaus used the nigh-imperceptible sound of Purple Ant's footsteps to follow his trail. It would seem that he'd slipped into the Westport Building through the emergency exit in the back, then used the maintenance stairs to ascend the floors. The security guards were his stooges, too, but one word from Thea put a quick end to their attack.

"Stop."

Upon seeing her, they froze in flabbergasted shock. They returned to their senses a few seconds later, but that was plenty of time for Klaus to knock them out with his lightning-fast fists.

Thea bit her lip.

Just how many people have been waiting for the hero to show up?

For the Worker Ants, the suggestion Hearth had planted in them had been their lone ray of hope in a world of despair.

They had been subjected to excruciating pain and forced to kill people again and again. Absurd as the notion of a dark-haired girl coming to save them was, the mere idea must have shone brighter to them than anything else.

I need to save them. They're my enemies, and they're trying to kill me, but I need to save them.

Thea rushed up the building's external staircase.

The Worker Ants continued attacking them even there, but she and Klaus subdued all comers. The two of them reached the eighth floor at the same time.

That was the floor that housed the rooftop garden.

The forty-seven-story-tall Westport Building contained a variety of tourist attractions, and one of them was the garden on its eighth floor. It had been closed off throughout the Tolfa Economic Conference, and between that and the late hour, there was nobody around.

The rooftop garden was roughly the size of three tennis courts. It had a fountain on its east and west sides, each of which was surrounded by a bed of roses, and there was a bronze monument enshrined in the garden's center. The monument depicted a goddess nurturing a dove that was about to take flight.

Purple Ant was waiting for them beneath the statue.

"This is where you want to make your stand?" Klaus asked.

"It is. And it was so thoughtful of you to come here all on your own, I must add." Purple Ant tenderly stroked the statue. "This is the same goddess as the one over in the harbor. Have you gotten a chance to visit it yet? They say she's a symbol of liberty; the statue celebrates how the immigrants who came here won their independence."

"I suppose that makes her your polar opposite."

"That it does. I despise her, you know. It makes me sick every time I have to look at her." Purple Ant extended his hand toward Klaus and Thea. "That's why I thought it would be apropos to kill you two right in front of her."

The moment the words left his mouth, a group of people rushed out from behind the rose beds. Thea could make out three of them, and they were all pointing their guns at her and Klaus.

"Ah!"

She tried to back off, but Klaus was faster. He leaped backward in an instant and yanked on her clothes to get her out of their line of fire.

Bullets whizzed right in front of her face.

Their assailants' timing and aim were impeccable.

The attackers gathered in front of Purple Ant. There were nine of them in total, each one clad in a tuxedo. Their ranks were comprised of men and women of all ages. One was a girl who'd barely left childhood, and another was a man on the verge of decrepitude. There was everything from housewives to young men in the prime of their youth. The only thing they all had in common was the dull look in their eyes.

"Say hello to my nine General Ants." Purple Ant smiled proudly. "They are my trump card."

He sat down on the statue's pedestal as if it were his throne.

Klaus fired his revolver. Thea hadn't even seen him draw it. Before the bullet could strike Purple Ant, though, his minions intercepted it. Two of them held up something that looked like shields and protected him.

Klaus let out an impressed murmur. "I can see they put your rank and file to shame."

"Oh, that they do," Purple Ant replied coolly. "I have more than four hundred Worker Ants, and these nine are the cream of the crop."

Thea acted fast. **"Stop right there,"** she said.

However, the General Ants didn't so much as twitch. She hadn't gotten through to them at all.

They must not have ever met Ms. Hearth. And because of the way they've been isolated, they never heard the rumor, either.

Those nine really were Purple Ant's ace in the hole. They were warriors through and through, and their sole charge was to defend the king.

Klaus gently nudged Thea back. "Stand down."

If her voice didn't work on them, all she was going to do was get in his way. It pained her to have to do so, but she fell back to the garden's entrance.

Purple Ant snapped his fingers.

With that as their signal, the nine General Ants swooped at Klaus as one. They readied their various weapons—one had a knife, another a rapier—and moved to surround him.

"____"

Klaus parried one woman's rapier thrust with his knife and moved to smash the butt of his gun against the back of her neck. However, he halted his attack at the last moment and leaped to the side instead. A bullet slammed into the ground where his feet had just been and bounced up off the concrete. A short distance away from the two of them, the old man was holding a rifle.

The moment Klaus escaped the old man's line of fire, a pair of boys charged at him and swung their longswords.

They're going to get him!

Right as that thought threatened to turn to a certainty in Thea's mind, though, Klaus fell back in the nick of time once more.

Something fluttered down on the garden. It was the scraps of Klaus's sleeve.

Purple Ant gave the battle's proceedings a satisfied nod. "I heard about the incident, you know. About how you let my teammate White Spider get away from you back in Din."

"........."

Klaus stared down at his tattered sleeve in silence.

Atop his pedestal, Purple Ant looked as composed as could be. "The reason was simple. You had no intel on young Spider, whereas he knew all about you. He knew everything from your upbringing to your strengths, your weaknesses, and how to beat you."

"It would certainly seem that way."

"A spy with their information leaked can't possibly hope to win."

As Purple Ant finished his speech, the General Ants resumed their attack.

Their coordination was impeccable. One of them thrust out their knife, and as they did, they were joined by a gunshot that soared right under their armpit. Klaus countered with a low kick, but another General Ant swooped in to block it, then brought their sword crashing down on his head.

It was like they were a single living organism.

Their eighteen eyes and eighteen hands moved about in perfect sync, allowing them to attack and defend at the same time.

It boggled the mind just thinking about how much time they must have spent training. It wasn't the kind you could count in days. Theirs was the kind of state you could only arrive at by having a prodigy sacrifice everything else in their life and spend ten thousand, perhaps even twenty thousand hours to attain. If not for Purple Ant's domination, it never would have been achieved.

Even so, Thea still couldn't believe her eyes.

Teach is actually getting overwhelmed?

Klaus's combat skills were second to none, and yet, all he was doing was defending himself.

Somewhere in her heart, Thea had harbored a baseless hope. *It's Teach,* she had thought. *Nine-on-one is no problem for him. Why, he could have taken on a hundred foes at once and emerged just as victorious.*

That was why she was having such difficulty processing the sight she was seeing.

How could it be?

"Sure enough, there it is. It's just like the intel said." As Thea stared in bewilderment, Purple Ant began talking. His voice had a smug superiority to it. "You're worried about your team, aren't you? About how they might be dying at this very moment."

"____!"

Thea's eyes went wide.

She assumed he was just bluffing, but looking at Klaus's movements, it did feel as though they lacked their usual shine. He was successfully weathering the General Ants' flawless tag-team attacks, but that was as far as he was getting.

Sweat ran across Klaus's face.

Could it be? Could an elite spy like him really be...shaken?

Thea frowned, unable to reconcile Klaus's performance with his abilities.

"There's this funny story I heard," Purple Ant said provocatively. "Apparently, they used to call you a king, too."

All the while, the General Ants continued their barrage.

"You lived in a war-ravaged slum as an orphan without parents or even a name," Purple Ant went on. "The only way you staved off starvation was by stealing food from gangs. The thing was, you were such a tough little brat, it creeped everyone else out. So you lived alone in a dirty, dusty garbage dump. That's why they called you the Dust King."

".........."

"The day you got taken in by a spy was the first time you ever had allies to call your own. It's touching; it really is. But it left you with a glaring weakness—you love your teammates like they're your family." Purple Ant gave him a pitying look. "It was traumatic, wasn't it? Losing your team the way you did."

That was when the balance shifted.

One of the General Ants managed to slip through Klaus's guard and charge at his flank. The Ant's fist slammed deep into his side. Klaus twisted his body to blunt the attack, but a look of anguish flitted across his face all the same.

That was the first blow Thea had ever seen him suffer.

Klaus quickly dashed backward and put some space between himself and his opponent.

The General Ants stopped attacking for a moment. They realized they had the upper hand, and they knew there was no need to rush things.

They simply adjusted their formation with a mechanical emotionlessness. They never offered Klaus even the slightest of openings.

"You should never have let yourself build another team," Purple Ant said. "You should have lived like a king. All you needed were slaves you could sacrifice at your whim. That way, you wouldn't have become weak."

Purple Ant had yet to so much as stir from his position atop the pedestal.

He merely watched with a sadistic gaze as Klaus grew more and more worn out.

"Teach..."

Thea recalled what he'd been like during their initial meeting. Back when she first arrived at Heat Haze Palace, his eyes had been so full of sorrow, they nearly looked frozen, and he'd devoted every minute of his free time to painting a piece he'd titled *Family*.

After losing his team, he had fought all by his lonesome.

But then he founded Lamplight. He had chosen to take them under his wing as their boss and as their instructor. From there, both teacher and students alike overcame hardships, trained tirelessly, and, in the end, completed their Impossible Mission.

The days they'd spent together had given the girls so many blessings.

The question was, what had they given Klaus?

"Why not just give up?" Purple Ant asked. "You couldn't beat my General Ants on your best day. With your mind off somewhere else, you don't stand a chance."

The situation was tilted against Klaus in every way possible. Having his information leaked had allowed Purple Ant to prepare the perfect stage on which to fight him.

A surge of anxiety ran through Thea. Klaus dusted off his clothes under her nervous gaze. "You really enjoy the sound of your own voice, don't you?" he said.

He sounded just as self-assured as always. Not even being boxed in by nine fierce foes was enough to cow him.

"I do feel bad about bringing this up after all that thoughtful monologuing, but you have it so wrong, I can't take it anymore. The only emotion I've been feeling is dejection from how tedious this all is."

Purple Ant raised an eyebrow. "Tedious? What are you talking about?"

Klaus let out a deep sigh. "To be blunt, I'm bored."

"What?"

"You certainly made your Nine General Ants *sound* impressive, but it's the exact same thing you were doing before. It's like you're fixated on this idea of finding strong people, using numbers to take them down, and making them your allies. Where's the innovation?"

"........."

Purple Ant froze, like he was struck speechless.

The thing was, Klaus had a point.

Purple Ant's ability was powerful, but it was the only trick he had. All he knew how to do was dominate people and sic them on his foes. The tactic's simplicity was what made it strong, but at the end of the day, that was all it was. Nothing more, nothing less.

Could that be the key?

As Thea tried to infer what exactly Klaus was getting at, her teacher went on coldly. "For all the hundreds of minions you have, all they're doing is carrying out a single man's worth of ideas. I have to say, it makes for a pretty uninteresting kingdom."

It all tied back to what Klaus himself had said. Or rather, to the lesson he'd passed along from Hearth.

"Differences between allies are the key to a strong organization," she'd said.

Klaus turned around. "Wouldn't you agree, Thea?"

"........."

The sudden question caught her by surprise.

After missing a beat, she realized what he was after.

"Oh, absolutely," she replied with a smile. "Why, he couldn't have made it easier to lead you around by the nose if he'd wanted to."

Purple Ant pressed down on the skin around his eyes in irritation. "I don't know what nonsense you're on about"—he snapped his fingers— "but if that's what you want your dying words to be, then so be it. **Take the girl hostage.**"

The General Ants sprang into action once more.

This time, they changed up their attack pattern. Seven of them went after Klaus, and the remaining two went after Thea as she watched the fight from the entrance. The twin boys bore down on her, longswords in hand.

Naturally, Thea stood no chance against them, and Klaus was too tied down to save her in time.

However, Thea could hear a familiar pair of footsteps charging up the stairs.

"You know, I can't imagine Teach is too pleased with me." The swords were moments from reaching her throat. "Not after I recruited *him* onto our side."

The footsteps reached their floor.

Her mighty bodyguard had finally arrived.

"I have a job for you," she said with a sweetly smile. **"Protect me."**

The General Ant twins froze in unison.

There was a man standing right in front of Thea, and he was grabbing the two Ants by their throats. He raised his emaciated arms into the air and hoisted the twins off their feet.

"Much appreciated." Thea gave him another smile. "And splendidly done, at that."

"You're too kind," Roland replied.

He threw his two foes with all his might and dashed them against the sculpture in the fountain.

"___"

Purple Ant gawked in disbelief.

On some level, though, he must have already realized it. After all, how else could Klaus have found his hideout?

As it turned out, there was one other suggestion Hearth had planted.

"I assume there's no need for introductions," Thea said. She gently stroked Roland's chin.

"After all, he's the man Ms. Hearth met right before she died—your dear pet dog."

One hour earlier...

"You're not the brightest, are you, kid? I can't believe you fell for it that easily."

Roland, now freed, squeezed down on Thea's throat. As his fingers dug into her skin, she arrived at a hypothesis.

It was about what her teammates had put their lives on the line to investigate—the hero of Mitario.

Whoever started that rumor had to work in a field where they might run into Purple Ant's Worker Ants, and they also had to know about the promise Thea made. There was only one person who that was true of—Hearth.

The reports said she had been killed by Serpent, so it stood to reason that Purple Ant could easily have been the one to do the deed there in Mitario. And right before Hearth died, she had planted a suggestion in his Worker Ants.

But was the story about the hero the only seed she had lain?

No... There's someone else involved in all this who's been acting strangely as well.

They had known since before the mission even began that he had ties to Purple Ant. And now that she thought about it, Klaus had expressed his confusion about the man's odd behavior as well.

Someone fed him that bald-faced lie *about being able to become Klaus's rival.*

Now everything finally made sense. All that time, Hearth had had everyone dancing in the palm of her hand.

She had known that Klaus would put together a new team after she died, she knew that he would find Thea, and because of the lies she told Roland, she knew that he would eventually challenge Klaus and get trounced. On top of that, she knew that Roland would sing like a bird and that Klaus and Thea would go after Purple Ant. She had accounted for all of it.

As far as destinies went, being the centerpiece of a legendary spy's final plan wasn't a half-bad one.

Thea strained her throat.

"Tell me, do you recognize my voice?"

Roland froze on the spot.

It hadn't been an intentional choice on her part, but Thea had never spoken clearly around him. Up until then, she had been too scared to hold a proper conversation with him, and because of that, he didn't know what her voice sounded like.

It was time to use that to her advantage.

She knew his weaknesses. He was sloppy, he was arrogant, and the moment he was certain he'd won, he left himself wide open. That was why, although unfastening his restraints had been a dangerous gamble, she hadn't had a choice but to do so.

"Stop right there," she said in Hearth's voice.

Roland was clearly shaken by that. At long last, it gave her an opening.

Thea slipped out of his hand, grabbed his face, and closed in. She held his head close enough for a kiss and locked her gaze on his.

"I'm code name Dreamspeaker—and it's time to lure them to their ruin."

She stared him deep in the eyes.

She could see his desires—what his sinister assassin heart was burdened by and what he craved. She etched it into her mind. Thanks to the ability Hearth had helped her hone, all of Roland's secrets were hers.

Roland shook off his stiffness and shoved her away. "Why, you little..."

Thea reached out and pressed her arms against the wall for balance to keep herself from toppling out the window. Then she rolled to the side and put some distance between them.

Her hair fluttered glossily behind her.

"I see, I see. You were there, weren't you? You watched Hearth die."

Thea had seen his heart, and she had seen the impression Hearth's dying words had left on it.

The suggestion Hearth had planted in him was a powerful one indeed.

"So what if I did?" Roland snapped his fingers. "It doesn't change the fact you're about to die. That's what I do. I kill."

The raw bloodlust he was emanating was enough to send pins and needles across her skin. Thea had been cowed by that menacing aura on multiple occasions. She had been completely helpless during their initial encounter, and the same thing had happened in the prison cell. Each time, she had needed one of her teammates to step in and protect her.

Now, though, she was different. Now she had a white-hot fire burning in her chest.

"And when you kill me, what then?"

The moment he wanted to, Roland could kill her faster than she could blink. Nobody was coming to save her. Yet, even so, Thea's smile was as elegant as could be. "Please, do tell. What good will killing me do you?"

"What are you—?"

"Oh, that's right. Purple Ant will praise you, won't he? That's very important. That way, you won't have to get punished."

"......!"

Roland's face flushed scarlet. She'd hit the nail on the head.

Thea playfully laid a finger on the corner of her mouth and smiled. "That's a real nice relationship you two have going on. *I worked real hard, so please don't hit me.* What are you going to do next, lick his feet? Oh, goodness, have you actually licked them? What a good little doggy you are."

"Listen here, kid. You little *bitch*..." His fists were trembling, and he was red all the way down to his fingertips. "You've got a hell of a lot of nerve. If you thought you were gonna die painlessly, well, think ag—"

"You know, I've been wondering this for a while, but why do you put on such a tough-guy act? I mean, you're a nobody. Teach took you down like it was nothing, and between that and the way you suck up to Purple Ant, you're really kind of pathetic." Thea looked at him coldly. "I don't think you understand who you really are, so allow me to tell you." She pointed at him and fired off each of her next words like they were bullets. "You're a haughty, weak narcissist who loves to leech off women. You suck up to your superiors, and you got broken in like a dog by some kinky S&M. You're no match for anyone with any *real* skills, but you let the fact that you're kind of decent at hunting fellow losers go to your head anyway. But at the end of the day, you're just a bargain-bin murderer without even the tiniest amount of brains or panache."

"Shut up..."

"Or what, you'll kill me? Let me ask you again—then what? Will you go back to the tedium of being Purple Ant's dog? If you do, it'll mean going back to traveling the world and killing whoever he tells you to while spending every day bored out of your mind. Then, one day, you'll pick a fight with the wrong guy and end up dead. Ha-ha-ha, and don't think you won't. I mean, it's not like you're actually *strong* or anything."

"Shut up… You don't know shit about me…"

"Oh, quit the barking and baying. A pathetic mutt like you who doesn't have the nerve to defy his owner or the patience to put up with his own boredom has no right filling my nose with his foul breath."

Thea laughed mockingly as she turned a deaf ear to Roland's attempts at defending himself.

Roland's body shook. He was still as red as a tomato, and his eyes swam like he was having a breakdown.

However, Thea didn't let up. She renounced his personality. She renounced his life. She renounced his very existence. She needed to break the domination Purple Ant had over him, and that was something that love alone couldn't accomplish. The only way she could do it was by facing him head-on.

What she was doing was replacing physical abuse with verbal abuse. She was violating his mind just the way Purple Ant had. However, Purple Ant's sole aim was to get his victims to submit to him. Thea's was not.

"But that's why your heart skipped a beat with excitement, wasn't it?" she asked him. "When that legendary Ms. Hearth swore to you that Klaus could satisfy your heart, you felt like it was destiny at work, didn't you? You were overjoyed at the prospect of finally having a proper rival, weren't you?"

"………"

"You want to change who you are so badly, you can taste it."

Back when they first met, Roland had complained incessantly about how bored he was. It was like he'd been cursing himself.

He was sick and tired of being controlled by Purple Ant.

Then she threw another piece of information in his face. "Why was it you helped out Olivia?"

Olivia was Roland's apprentice, the one who'd disguised herself as a maid and gotten captured by Grete. Now she, too, was locked away in a prison and being pumped for all the intel she had, but originally, she had worked as a lady of the night.

The way Olivia saw it, running into Roland was what had saved her from a life of boredom and drudgery.

"Was it really just so you could use her as a pawn? Or was it because you sympathized with her plight? You saw so much of yourself in her, didn't you? That's why you wanted to save her."

"........."

"You know, if you switch sides to the Republic now, you could win her back her freedom."

She was facing him with all her cards on the table. It was time to take the information she'd gathered and put it together so she could win him over. Her heart sang with a firm sense of purpose. This, she now realized, was the role she'd been given.

Last time, her attempt to become a hero who saved even her enemies had ended in disaster. Her opponent had taken advantage of her empathy, and Thea had made the terrible blunder of helping her escape. The weight of that failure had been too much for her heart to bear.

But the thing was, she'd been going about it all wrong. There *was* a way for spies to save their foes, and it wasn't by letting them get away. It was by *getting them to turn traitor*. All she had to do was turn her enemies into allies!

That was the way Dreamspeaker was going to operate—by denouncing her foes, then using her charm to lure them onto her side.

"Even if that's true...," Roland eventually said in a pained voice, "what exactly can *you* do?"

"I can liberate you. With my power to see into your heart, I can free you from Purple Ant's control."

She had seen it etched into his heart. He, too, believed that the dark-haired heroine was coming to save him. All he wanted was to be set free, and she was the person who could do just that.

"Or if you'd like me to put it another way...shall I do a bit of home-wrecking?"

She gave Roland a soft push, and he fell backward onto the ground like his spine was made of jelly. He looked up at her in blank astonishment.

Thea sat down on the bed and stripped off her shoes.

"Go on, kneel before your new owner."

She stroked his chin with her bare, ever-so-fair feet. She could feel his breath hot and heavy on them.

* * *

"Now, do you want to experience the best kind of pleasure there is together with your beautiful mistress?"

It didn't take long at all for Roland to succumb to that smile of hers.

Back on the Westport Building's eighth-floor rooftop garden...

"Y'know, I'd always wanted to see how many Worker Ants I could take down in a single go." Roland loudly cracked his neck. "Turns out, I'm pretty good at this stuff. I took out twelve of those punks, no problem. Not being allowed to kill 'em made it a whole lot trickier, but still, that number's competitive with anything those foreign intelligence agencies put up."

Purple Ant gave Roland a frigid glare, but Roland didn't seem bothered in the slightest. He'd probably been just as unflappable his whole life. He twirled Thea's gun around in his hand.

The arrival of an intruder caused the General Ants to back off for a bit, and Roland took advantage of that opening to give Klaus an over-familiar shout. "I saved those kids of yours, Bonfire. You can stop worrying about 'em."

Klaus didn't seem one bit pleased.

It was clear how deeply he detested Roland, but at the same time, the fact he owed the man some gratitude was undeniable.

As Thea looked back and forth between the two of them, another newcomer showed up behind her.

"Hey there. I see you finally figured out how to make yourself useful."

It was Monika. Being reunited with her teammate sent a wave of relief through Thea. "Oh, thank goodness you're alive."

"Yeah, we're all fine. Klaus went and saved Lily and Annette, and the Corpse guy bailed out Sybilla and Erna. Oh, and also—"

Midway through her matter-of-fact explanation, one of Monika's veins bulged. She grabbed Thea by the collar.

"—you got anything you wanna say to me? About that giant load you dumped on my back, maybe? The only backup we got was Grete in a disguise. Bet you thought that'd be real funny, huh? I swear, I was *this* close to losing it when I found out it was her."

"I mean, you *did* make it out alive..."

"Only 'cause I worked my ass off!"

"A-and besides, that deployment was Grete's idea..."

"Says the commander who signed off on it."

The bottom line was, they had successfully weathered Purple Ant's three simultaneous crises without suffering a single casualty.

Monika and Sara were the duo Thea had been most worried about, but as it turned out, Grete's valiant efforts had paid off. By disguising herself as Klaus and giving their opponents a good scare, she'd given Monika an opportunity to outplay them.

Thanks to her and Roland, everyone had made it out alive. The other girls were gathered out on the external stairs as well. Their target, Purple Ant, had nowhere to run.

"Anyway," Monika went on, "all we managed to do is get away. We didn't take down a single one of 'em. You should be thankful I'm such a genius."

"Oh, trust me, I am."

"And there's nothing we can do here, either. At this point, whether or not we succeed"—Monika shot a look over at Klaus and Roland—"rests entirely on those two."

The two spies whose backs she was looking at were on a level far beyond anything the girls had reached.

There was "Bonfire" Klaus.

And there was "Deepwater" Roland.

Even though Thea was the one who'd helped bring it about, she still felt a bit awed by the sight. There was nothing more she or the others could contribute.

The two elite spies bantered as they stood side by side.

"...Roland, I appreciate you saving my subordinates. You have my gratitude."

"What? C'mon, why can't you just say *thank you* like a normal person? Remember, if it wasn't for me turning traitor, you never would've found Purple Ant's hideout."

"Please, you betrayed one man. Try not to let it go to your head."

Across from them, Purple Ant sat with his eyes twitching and his nine underlings surrounding him. Unable to conceal his displeasure, he dug his nails into one of the General Ant boys' backs.

"Still," Klaus said, "there's one thing I should say. You aren't—"

"Don't," Roland cut him off. "There're some things a guy's just gotta do. This here, this is me taking back my life."

"Hmm?" Thea couldn't understand what they were getting at.

Klaus said nothing more. He merely fixed his gaze on Purple Ant.

"..."

A stillness fell as both sides tried to feel the other out.

Before Thea realized it, she was holding her breath. The tension of it all was so intense it made her feel faint, but she managed to pull herself together.

Beside her, Monika was watching the proceedings like a hawk. She was planning on learning everything she could from the battle, and she refused to miss so much as a second of it. As far as straight-up fights to the death went, what they were about to witness was the apex of spy combat.

The first person to make a move was Purple Ant.

He rose to his feet and thrust his finger at Klaus and Roland.

"All units," his voice boomed. **"Kill the traitor first."**

The nine General Ants moved as one and charged at Roland, who readied his gun.

They were completely ignoring Klaus, and Klaus took the opportunity to fire off some shots. His bullets pierced two of the nine through their shoulders. However, they didn't so much as flinch, and their coordination remained impeccable. All of them, including the two who'd just been injured, began their assault on Roland.

They rained a succession of rapier thrusts, longsword slashes, and gunshots upon their gaunt foe.

Roland opened fire with the gun he'd borrowed from Thea.

"What...?" Thea gasped.

She couldn't believe what she was witnessing.

The long and short of it was, Roland was completely and utterly outmatched.

He managed to wound the first man who dove at him with his signature quickdraw technique, but when one of the women swooped in from the side with a series of rapier strikes, he was too slow to react.

The woman stabbed him in the flank, and when he recoiled, a bullet caught him right in the gut.

Then the two sword-wielding twins swooped in to finish the job and hacked away at both his legs in unison.

"Ro...land...?"

She could tell just how serious his injuries were.

His entire body gushed blood as the General Ants kicked him aside and returned to their formation.

Thea hurriedly rushed to his side, but he was already too badly hurt to even move. The bullet hole in his abdomen looked especially grim. She administered first aid, but it was anyone's guess as to whether or not that would be enough to keep him alive.

"A fitting end for a man who defied his king," Purple Ant declared coldly. "There was no way a man of his paltry talents could ever stand up to my General Ants."

Thea said nothing. There was something she'd just been forcibly reminded of.

Roland may have been talented, but there were people more powerful still who could trounce people like him like it was nothing. Klaus may have held his own against the General Ants, but that was only because he was an anomaly. Even Roland, skilled as he was in combat, was no match for them.

Klaus was the only person who could even hope to face them.

"I must admit," Purple Ant said, "I made a few miscalculations this time around. I'll give you props for that. However, this all falls well within my margins of error. My victory is still just as assured."

Purple Ant pressed his stun gun up to one of the injured General Ants.

A scream rose up, as did the smell of burning flesh. He had cauterized the Ant's wound.

After going around and applying his violent treatment to the rest of his injured peons, he began explaining himself with great delight. "Your mentor told us everything about you, young Klaus, and our very own Spider verified that intelligence with his own two eyes. Even if you were in peak condition, you wouldn't hold a candle to my General Ants."

Klaus said nothing. ".........."

"A king gives no quarter to traitors. Now it's time for the rest of you to die, too. You and the children hiding over on the stairs."

Klaus's silent gaze was fixed on Roland's prone form. Thea continued doing her best to patch him up, but he just kept on losing more and more blood.

Eventually, Klaus looked back at Purple Ant. "Would you mind if I asked you a question?" He fixed his gaze straight on his foe. "I despise that corpse of a man. He may have just been following orders, but he still killed scores of innocent people. And what's more, he knew this was going to happen when he chose to duke it out with you. I don't feel sorry for him in the slightest."

"Well, that certainly makes two of us," Purple Ant replied.

"Even so, wasn't he your teammate? Your compatriot?"

"Please. He was a slave."

"Ah. You know, you really are a sickening man."

Klaus began advancing forward, and the nine General Ants sprang into action as well.

The former's goal was to reposition himself so that Thea and the others wouldn't get caught up in the fight. One of the General Ants took a potshot at Thea in an attempt to distract Klaus, but Monika swatted the bullet out of the air.

That was enough to show their opponents that diversionary tactics weren't going to get them anywhere.

It was time for the battle between Klaus and the General Ants to begin in earnest.

The Ants had suffered a fair number of blows, but their coordination was none the worse for it. Rapier and longsword tag-team attacks hammered down on Klaus, and bullets wove their way between the blades and whizzed at him as well. Whenever he tried to go in for a knife strike, one of the Ants in charge of defense would swoop in and block it with their shield.

Roland hadn't lasted three seconds against that pressure, and it wasn't because he was weak. The General Ants were just unreasonably strong.

Klaus had already lasted for more than a minute, but his breathing was starting to grow ragged. He had fought seventy-three Worker Ants on his way there, so it made sense that fatigue was starting to get to him.

The General Ants were pushing him back. It was only a bit at a time, but they were definitely gaining ground on him.

All Thea could do was cheer him on.

She shot him a wordless look of encouragement. Over in her peripheral vision, she could see the others. They, too, were watching the battle with their fists clenched and their gazes burning. They were praying for the same thing she was—for the instructor who'd guided them all to such heights to emerge victorious.

In defiance of those wishes, though, Klaus had to beat a large retreat.

Blood trickled down his cheek.

"Are you not listening?" Purple Ant asked. "I told you, we have a full dossier on you."

Klaus wiped away the blood. "………"

Purple Ant snapped his fingers. "Even if you were fighting at full strength, my General Ants are the one foe you can't beat. Now **kill him**."

There it was. The kill order.

The General Ants swooped in as one. Klaus was under attack from every side. All of them, even the marksman and the ones on shield duty, were on offense now.

The nine of them were in perfect sync.

From Klaus's right, the old man bore down on him at point blank with his rifle. From the front, the twins charged in with their longswords. From his left, two men raised their shields to use as bludgeons. From behind him, a woman made to run him through with her rapier. And the others filled in the little gaps with their guns and swords and knives. Klaus was surrounded.

"I see. Well, then I should ask…"

Klaus's voice rang out.

It was those same words the girls had heard him say so many times before.

"…how much longer should I keep playing along with this game?"

He dodged through the General Ants' onslaught by the slimmest of margins like he'd read them like a book. Then he shifted his leg, and the sound of gas spraying filled the air. Klaus had installed some sort of device in his shoe. He covered his nose and mouth with a handkerchief.

The General Ants lost their balance. They were still acting in perfect harmony, and as a result, all nine of them sucked in their breath in unison—just in time to get a big lungful of gas.

"Poison gas...?" Purple Ant muttered in bewilderment. "But there wasn't anything in your file about you using—"

Thea knew that gas.

It was the poison gas Lily always used. The timing Klaus released it with was even more perfect than hers, offering his foes no openings whatsoever as he used the paralytic to dull all their movements in one fell swoop.

The sight Thea saw next was one she would never forget.

It didn't even take a full second. There was a big old zero to the left of that decimal place.

In that moment, the man who boasted of being the World's Strongest showed what he was truly capable of.

He stepped forward and traveled several feet in what seemed like an instant.

As he did, *six of the General Ants went flying.*

The way Klaus's assailants got launched into the air like scraps of paper before landing hard on the ground, it was like an invisible bomb had gone off or something.

At that point, Thea realized that she'd had it all wrong.

Klaus had never been up against the ropes, not even at the very beginning. Sure, he had been worried about his team. And sure, that might have hampered his performance. But any change that had brought about was little more than a rounding error. He had known all along how he was going to bring his foes low.

What he'd been doing was figuring out when the best time to release his poison gas was.

The weakness he'd shown had simply been an act.

"Let me point out where you made your mistake," Klaus said. "You got all sorts of intel on me from my master's betrayal, yes, but that information is six months out of date. In a time frame like that, even my skill set is going to grow."

"B-but it doesn't make sense…," Purple Ant stammered, still failing to come to grasps with the situation. "Just last month—"

"Oh, you mean when I let White Spider get away? That much is true; I won't deny it. The only cop-out excuse I have to give is that at the time, I was in terrible form. I'd been working for more than five hundred days straight at that point."

That was hardly a cop-out.

Grete had noticed his poor condition as well. After leading them to success during the bioweapon retrieval mission in Galgad, he'd spent their subsequent two-week vacation wearing himself out by completing more missions still. Then, without taking a moment to rest, he'd headed off to assassinate Corpse. And to top it all off, he'd pounded no shortage of pavement in his search for the missing girls.

During his encounter with White Spider, he must have been exhausted.

"When White Spider ran into me, he misunderstood. He saw me at my weakest, and it made him think that that old intel was still accurate."

Klaus went on.

"Unfortunately for you, I've become far stronger than I was half a year ago."

Klaus took another step forward, and the remaining three General Ants went flying as well.

He was moving, and he was attacking. That was all there was to it, but due to Klaus's speed, it really did look like his foes were getting blasted away by invisible explosions.

The secrets to Klaus's talent were his extraordinary combat techniques and the raw power he had that allowed him to boast of being the World's Strongest. Or at least, that's what Thea had thought they were.

Now, though, a new thought crossed her mind.

Could it be? Is his real talent the way he learns?

Perhaps that was another gift of his—the ability to pick up new skills off intuition alone.

Thea shuddered.

We threw everything we had at him over and over. We tried putting him into all sorts of different situations, and we attacked him with the most ingenious plans we could think up. Could Teach have been using that to train himself, *too?*

The girls' talents were far from outstanding, but each of them had one specific skill they could use better than anyone. They had used those skills to their fullest in their attacks, so their attempts couldn't have been *that* mediocre.

Because of that, Klaus had been forced to live like he could get attacked at any moment, no matter where he was. He had been forced to anticipate traps of every sort. And he had seen the girls' unique skills up close and personal.

It begged the question, just what exactly had a man with his superhuman talents been getting out of the time they'd spent together?

"Now then," Klaus said as he shook the dust off his hands. "Are you ready to do this, Purple Ant?"

He gave his opponent a coolheaded stare.

There was nobody left to defend Purple Ant. He could spout off all the orders he wanted to, but there wasn't a single person who would rise up to obey them.

Furthermore, it went without saying that he didn't stand a chance against Klaus one-on-one. The battle was over, and the girls were blocking off his escape route. Without his minions, they had nothing to fear from him.

Purple Ant could see the writing on the wall. He inched backward, but he soon bumped up against the statue's pedestal. Great beads of sweat began rolling down his face.

"You have to help me." He sounded downright pathetic. "You want to save your enemies, don't you? Please talk some sense into him."

Thea could tell that she was the one he was talking to.

The expression on his face was pleading and desperate. It was hard to imagine this was the same person who'd been calling himself a king. Without his subjects, a king was just a man.

"Even I understand that there are people who are worth saving and people who aren't," Thea replied flatly.

That was something she was confident of. Purple Ant was beyond salvation. His personality was rotten to its core, and she knew better than to hope he would ever change.

"You're like a walking natural disaster," she went on. "Enemies are one thing, but you're so repugnant, I hesitate to call you even that."

Klaus started approaching Purple Ant. As he did, he pulled out a bullet from his pocket. It was the memento Hearth had left. Purple Ant went pale, and Klaus squeezed his hand around the bullet as he walked right up to him.

Thea did the verbal honors.

"The fact of the matter is, you aren't qualified to be our enemy."

Klaus took his fist with Hearth's bullet in it and smashed it into Purple Ant's face.

The man fell unconscious without even getting a chance to scream. With that, Mitario's king was deposed.

Epilogue
Boss and Graduation

Their mission in Mitario may have been complete, but there were still some odds and ends they needed to attend to.

Lamplight had fought their hardest, and the results they'd put up had been impressive indeed. However, that victory came at a price.

They paid that toll right as Klaus was tying up Purple Ant's unconscious body.

A wave of hostility washed over them, and a bullet ripped through the night sky. That was no lead bullet. That was a rifle round. Even for the mighty Klaus, dodging it took everything he had. As he did, the sensation reminded him of someone.

It reminded him of the sniper who'd killed his mentor Guido.

The spy in question didn't hesitate to kill his own allies if it meant protecting his secrets.

Two more shots sounded out.

Klaus deflected the first one. After all the work it had taken to capture Purple Ant, he wasn't going to let him die that easily.

However, the second shot blew off a wholly unexpected target's right foot.

"Roland?" Thea gasped.

His battle with Purple Ant had left him too wounded to dodge.

Thea screamed, and Monika had to grab her sleeve to force her behind cover.

The sniper was too far away to make out with the naked eye, yet all their shots had flown with unerring accuracy. Thea had a faint idea of how much raw skill that must have taken.

A buzzer rang out from Purple Ant's breast pocket. He was carrying a radio on him. Klaus put it up to his ear and was greeted by a familiar voice.

"Screw off, you monster."

It was White Spider—another member of Serpent.

"I gotta say, I wasn't expecting you to capture my buddy Purple Ant alive. Not gonna lie, that's kinda messed up."

"I see he wasn't working alone. How about that rematch, then?"

"Dude, you really gotta stop trying to bait me. I'm not about that life. Do I look like a guy with a death wish?"

It was obnoxious how flippant White Spider was being.

This time, though, it was Klaus who had the upper hand.

"We have Purple Ant in custody. Once we drag your information out of him, we'll know everything about you and your team."

"Nah, Purple Ant's not gonna talk. C'mon—give the guy some credit."

"We'll see about that."

"Well, best of luck with that. You guys had your hands so full dealing with Purple Ant, I was able to get my work done unopposed. I already got what I wanted here, and it's all thanks to him."

By the sound of it, White Spider had been doing espionage work at the Tolfa Economic Conference as well. However, Klaus had no idea what that might have been. The Worker Ants Purple Ant sent after him had taken up all his time.

"This round? This one's all yours," White Spider said. *"Next time, though, you're dead. You're getting to be a real pain in Serpent's butt. Seriously, we're gonna kill you. I'm done with this brute-force nonsense. I'm gonna look at every angle, work through all the details, and come up with a plan that'll put you down for good."*

"'You're dead,' 'We're gonna kill you'... What are you, a child? You really need to start carrying yourself with some dignity."

"Shut up, man. Leave my personality out of this."

"What's Serpent even after anyway? There's no way you're just a bunch of Imperial loyalists."

"*What makes you say that?*"

"Because if you were, my master would have never joined you."

White Spider's laughter crackled over the radio. "*Why don't you ask Purple Ant? If you can get him to talk, that is.*"

"........."

"*If I had to describe it...I'd say we're after balance.*"

The radio signal went dark, and the prickly feeling of hostility vanished from the air. White Spider was gone.

He was an inscrutable one, that White Spider. He acted like a two-bit goon, and he'd clearly been scared of Klaus, but then he'd gone on to boast and brag, and his final words had been pregnant with significance. It was impossible to tell if he was incredibly powerful or unimaginably weak. The only real impression he'd left was of how difficult to read he was.

The moment the sniper's presence vanished, Thea rushed out from her hiding spot.

"Roland!"

He was still alive, but his leg was in tatters and his face was ghastly pale. His eyes had a hollow, lightless look to them.

The girls gathered around him.

"I..." Sybilla knelt down by his side. "This guy saved my life. Erna and I woulda been dead if he hadn't shown up when he did."

Klaus looked at the man wordlessly. "........."

Meanwhile, Thea tried desperately to keep Roland alive, tearing off strips of her clothes so she could use them to bind his wounds. He had tried to kill her on two different occasions, and yet here she was, attempting to save him yet again.

"Thea," Klaus called to her, "that's enough. He's too far gone."

Grete touched Thea's hand to urge her to stop applying first aid. Thea bit her lip and withdrew her hands from Roland's body.

When Klaus walked over, Roland's eyes twitched a little. "Bonfire..." His voice was almost too faint to hear.

"What?" Klaus replied.

"Tell me, do you think I ever could've become your rival?"

"..................."

It was clear what answer Roland wanted to hear. And Klaus could tell that the girls wanted him to say it, too.

However, his answer wasn't the one they'd been hoping for. "Not in a million years."

"...Well, damn."

"Did you expect me to console you? None of your wishes came true. All you ever did was follow orders and murder people. You accomplished nothing of renown, made no meaningful connections with others, and will die with no honor to your name. It's a fitting end for someone who's killed as many innocent people as you."

It was true that he'd saved Sybilla's and Erna's lives. However, that was far from enough to balance out everything he'd done in the past. The deeds he'd committed were unforgivable.

"That said," Klaus went on, "I would say you've earned yourself the right to have us give you a proper send-off."

"Hey, I'll take it. You know, it only lasted a moment, and maybe it was all just a sick joke, but I kinda enjoyed getting to fight by your side." Roland reached out into empty space. "And...Thea... Thanks... for saving me..."

Thea squeezed his feebly outstretched hand. The moment she touched him, the remnants of his strength faded, and Roland breathed his last.

Klaus offered up a silent prayer.

By all rights, he deserved a much worse death than that. The weight of his sins was immense. He should have gotten tortured to death in a prison where no light could reach. Either that or he should have died by his own hand on Purple Ant's orders. That was the destination his path as a spy should have ended at.

Considering all that, perhaps this was the closest thing to a happy ending he could've gotten.

Grete took a knife and gently cut off his shirt's collar. She intended to use it as a memento. After all, there was still a woman being held in a Din prison who loved Roland with all her heart.

After Annette doused the body in gasoline, Thea lit a match. "Goodbye, Roland."

The whole team watched solemnly as the blazing flames consumed his remains.

◇◇◇

A mere two hours after their climactic showdown, Klaus stood on a dock. That there was the gateway that connected the United States of Mouzaia to continents abroad. Even then, in the dead of night, there were passenger ships and freighters going in and out of the port without pause.

A large music case sat beside him. It had originally been designed to hold a cello, but now, Purple Ant lay unconscious within.

It was time to make good on an agreement.

At three AM, the person he was waiting for arrived.

It was a Black man wearing round glasses. Oddly, he was wearing the kind of robes one would expect to see on a priest. Based on how much of his hair had gone white, it wasn't hard to guess at his age.

"What are you here for?" the man asked quietly, to which Klaus replied succinctly.

"Candy and sweets."

That seemingly absurd exchange was a code designed to let them both know they were dealing with the right person.

"You're Bonfire, then." The man nodded. "I'm a runner from the JJJ. Please call me Corrector."

"Corrector it is."

"I've been hearing rumors about you for quite some time now. They say you're the best spy in the entire Din Republic."

"It feels kind of ironic, being a spy who gets gossiped about."

Klaus's reply earned him a muffled laugh from Corrector.

The JJJ was Mouzaia's intelligence agency in charge of all espionage and counterespionage across the vast United States. Officially speaking, they had an alliance with the Din Republic's Foreign Intelligence Office in the name of keeping an eye on the Galgad Empire.

"Purple Ant, you called him?" Corrector said, getting right down to business. "We were looking into this business about the spy killings over at the JJJ, too. So he was the mastermind behind it all? I lost a lot of colleagues to that man. I'm impressed you managed to take him down."

"Thank you. Supposedly, he's part of an Imperial intelligence group called Serpent. Have you heard of them?"

"No, this is all news to me. I wonder what their deal is?" Corrector pushed his glasses up his nose. "Now, you mentioned something about having us hold on to Purple Ant for you?"

"He won't come cheap, of course."

"What's your price?"

"Every piece of intelligence the JJJ has on Serpent. And don't give me that nonsense about not knowing who they are."

Corrector shrugged. "Fair enough. We at the JJJ have every desire to maintain a good working relationship with the Foreign Intelligence Office."

Klaus could instinctively tell that Corrector was telling the truth.

He agreed to hand Purple Ant over.

In all honesty, he was a little conflicted about doing so. Purple Ant could prove to be a highly valuable source of intelligence. However, Klaus doubted he was going to give up his information easily, and given that they were on foreign soil, the risks associated with transporting him and keeping him confined over long periods of time were too high to stomach. Handing him over to the United States to curry favor with them was the best option he had.

Klaus went on to list a few more conditions, including that the Republic be present whenever Purple Ant was tortured.

"By the way," Corrector said right before they parted ways, "rumor has it that your superior visited our neck of the woods, too. You know anything about that?"

"Not a thing. I was on a different op at the time."

Klaus himself had only just learned that Hearth had been operating in Mitario. In all likelihood, she'd been meddling with the Tolfa Economic Conference as well. It was odd, then, how the Din brass had told Klaus that Hearth had been part of the bioweapon retrieval mission.

Corrector shook his head. "Oy vey. You've got that, you've got Serpent... I don't understand what's going on in this world of ours anymore."

He took the cello case and left with a sigh.

Three days after the battle, the girls were all gathered in Thea's apartment.

Lily—never one for decorum—stood boldly atop the table, pointed out the window, and shouted at the top of her lungs. "Who's ready to go be tourists?!"

""""""Yeahhhhhhhh!""""""" the others cheered.

Their long battle against Purple Ant was finally over.

Sara looked at them in shock. "You all change gears really quickly…"

The mission had technically ended the moment they captured Purple Ant, but there had still been some odds and ends that needed to be taken care of afterward.

In particular, there was the matter of rehabilitating the Worker Ants who had suffered at Purple Ant's hands. Thea had played a big role in spearheading that effort. There had also been the matter of covering up the whole incident, and although Klaus had handled the negotiations with Mouzaia's intelligence agency, the JJJ, he had forced the girls to help out with some of the details.

Thanks to the JJJ's help, they were able to get a full list of the conference attendees that Purple Ant stationed Worker Ants with. One of them was almost certainly connected to whatever Serpent's objective was, but the team decided to hold off on digging through all the intel until they'd gotten home.

Lamplight had finished up the last of the work the night prior, and it was bright and early in the morning.

"Elite spies work hard, but we play hard, too," Lily replied.

With the mission finally finished, the girls were chomping at the bit to finally get in some sightseeing.

Then a knock echoed through the room, and Klaus popped inside. "We don't have time for that. We're leaving, and we're leaving now."

Lily looked at him aghast. "Wait, why?"

Klaus handed her an envelope. "The JJJ and I finished fine-tuning our cover-up. Tomorrow, the local police are going to make this report public."

The girls tilted their heads in confusion and unsealed the letter.

Upon skimming its contents, they all let out a unified "whoa…"

Lillian Hepburn, a waitress of unidentified origins working at the burger joint on the ground floor of the Westport Building, was suspected of murder. Upon being pulled aside for questioning, she dropped a gun and fled the scene. After leading the police on a chase and setting off bombs throughout the city, she ultimately burned herself to death atop the Westport Building's rooftop garden.

At this time, we believe she may have been connected to as many as seventy-six mysterious deaths.

"You made me out to be some sort of horrible monster!" Lily yelped. "Lillian Hepburn" was the alias she'd been using during their time in the States. "And what's with this *'seventy-six mysterious deaths'* part?!"

"The JJJ and I decided to tie the murders Purple Ant's committed over the past six months, the false charges levied against you, and the chaos you and Annette caused into one tidy little package."

"Have you no subtlety?!"

"The point is, we need to be out of the United States by the end of the day. As of tomorrow, you'll officially be dead."

Sightseeing would have to wait for another occasion. It was time for them to get the hell out of Mouzaia.

Later on, the Mitario police's report became the talk of the town. A mug shot that didn't look the slightest bit like Lily got plastered all over TV news broadcasts, and the story shocked the entire United States to its core.

All the general public knew was an evil woman named Lillian had died at the Westport Building after a prolonged standoff against the police, and in time, the tale took on a life of its own. By the time the legend of "Lillian the Devil" started getting passed down through the generations, the story had nothing to do with the real Lily whatsoever.

Nobody who heard it had any idea that Purple Ant had so much as existed.

On Lily's insistence, they decided to indulge themselves on the ferry ride back, and the whole team spent their weeklong voyage in reserved luxury cabins.

The moment they got to their rooms, the girls immediately began jumping on the beds, and it wasn't long before an all-out pillow fight erupted. Ultimately, the others decided to bury Erna in mattresses, and they all gathered around her and piled their bedding high atop the mound. The modern art they ended up with looked so much like Mitario's statue that they dubbed it the "Erna of Anti-Liberty."

As he looked around at the absolute mess the girls had made, Klaus realized that one of them was missing.

He walked around the ferry looking for her. On his way, he passed by a kiosk and bought some popcorn. Then, when he got to the upper deck, he spotted her standing under the clear blue sky.

Thea gazed out at the scenery.

The ferry had set sail, and the Mitario skyline was growing tinier by the moment. Those same buildings that had blown her away with their height as she had walked the city's streets now looked like little more than scale models.

The sea wind blew through her hair as she heard a voice from behind her. "Hello there, Thea."

"Teach..."

"What are you doing all alone up here? You and the others didn't get into a fight, did you?"

Klaus took a spot by Thea's side.

A flock of seagulls was flying abreast with the ferry. Klaus threw them some of his popcorn, and the birds deftly snatched it out of the air and flew off with it.

"Do you mind if I try?" Thea asked, so he handed her some. However, she had little success throwing it to them. Perhaps dexterity wasn't her strong suit.

Klaus gave her a gentle look. "You did a fantastic job on this mission. If not for you turning Roland, I wouldn't have been able to find Purple Ant."

"It's all thanks to the intel the others risked their lives to pull together. I couldn't have done it without them."

"Why go off on your own, then? If you're feeling sentimental and I'm being a bother, don't hesitate to tell me to leave."

Thea shook her head at his offer. "No, I just have a lot on my mind. Actually, I'm glad you came."

"Why's that?"

"I've been curious. What was Ms. Hearth like as a spy?"

So that was why she was gazing at Mitario. That was the city where a great spy had fallen.

Klaus paused for a good long while before answering. "She was a blazing fire of a woman. There were times when she was as warm as could be; there were times when she burned her enemies to the ground... I'm sorry. When I try to describe her, it all ends up coming out sort of abstract."

Klaus couldn't think of a way to succinctly sum up who she'd been, and he cursed his inability to explain things properly.

"Do you mind if this goes a little long?" he asked. "I feel like rather than describing her, it would be better if I recounted some anecdotes about her instead. And besides, we have nothing on this boat but time."

"Oh, that would be lovely. I could listen to stories about her all day and night," Thea said with a warm smile.

Then her eyes gleamed like she'd just had a fantastic idea.

"In fact, while we're here, why don't you tell me them all night long? That would really get the emotions flowing. If you come to my and Grete's room tonight, you can lie between us on the bed as you—"

"You never learn, do you?" Klaus said, massaging his temples. "Just for the record, I'll have you know there are men who don't enjoy it when conversations turn sexual."

"Oof. Monika told me the exact same thing."

"You should listen to your teammates' advice."

"Come to think of it, Sybilla and Sara have been getting together recently and holding meetings on how to convince Grete to stop listening to my teachings. Were you the one who put them up to that?"

"Nope. They're acting entirely out of the goodness of their hearts."

Apparently, Klaus wasn't the only one she was making problems for. Considering her position within the team, he wished she would put a little more common sense into her actions, but he recognized that there was no point hoping for the impossible.

Thea gave her shoulders a dejected slump. "*Sigh*... You know, Teach, I wouldn't mind if you started being a little nicer to me. We're birds of a feather, after all."

"We are? How so?"

"Isn't it obvious? We're the two people with vendettas against Serpent," she replied proudly.

Klaus had no rebuttal to that.

At the end of the day, not many of Lamplight's members had any personal stakes in the battle against Serpent. They all wanted to defend their nation, of course, but Klaus and Thea were the only two who'd had their savior murdered by the group.

"You don't have to carry it all alone anymore. I'm going to help you fight Serpent," Thea said, offering Klaus her hand. "Let's be partners, you and I."

"........."

Klaus was surprised.

Thea had always had lofty ideals, but historically, they hadn't really gotten her anywhere. Instead, the gulf between her ideals and reality usually caused her so much anguish that she ended up just following the rest of the team's lead.

Now, though, she was making her case to him by taking active steps forward.

"You really are the one who grew the most during this last mission," he remarked.

"I—I am? I mean, if you say so, but it really doesn't feel like I've—"

"Magnificent." Klaus grasped her hand in his. "I can see you're determined, and I respect that. Let's hunt down Serpent together."

"I'm looking forward to it."

Thea squeezed back, and the two of them shook on it.

Then Thea's cheeks went red. "W-we wouldn't want Grete to get the wrong impression," she said as she hurriedly let go of Klaus's hand. "I know I just said we should work together, but I think it would be best if I stopped acting so clingy around you."

"Probably, yes. I think that's an excellent—"

"After all, I have a duty to support my teammates in all their romantic endeavors! Not just Grete, no. If any of the others fall for you, I need to be ready to act as their love guru and give them all sorts of advice on how to—"

"I would recommend abdicating that duty posthaste," Klaus replied with a look of genuine displeasure. Thea laughed.

After that, the two of them shared a pleasant conversation. Fortunately, there was nobody else around, nor were there any signs the boat had been bugged, so Klaus got to regale her with his impressions of the rest of Inferno's members.

He told her all about Hearth, the team's boss, and about "Torchlight" Guido, the team's second-in-command and Klaus's personal mentor. Then he went on to tell her about "Firewalker" Gerde, their fierce old lady sniper; "Soot" Lukas and "Scapulimancer" Wille, the merry pair of brothers who loved playing games and gambling; and finally, about "Flamefanner" Heide, the de facto older sister of the team who had a sharp tongue and a side gig writing erotica.

As Klaus told Thea stories about his deceased teammates, she spoke up like she'd just remembered something. "Now that I think about it, I guess she never ended up getting to make good on that promise..."

"What promise is that?"

"The one Ms. Hearth made me. She told me that when we met again, she would prepare a wonderful present for me. I was really looking forward to it, too."

In the end, that reunion had never come, and Thea never got a chance to receive that gift.

Klaus placed his hand on his mouth and sank into thought. "........."

"Hmm? What's wrong, Teach?"

"Nothing, I was just thinking. The boss was big on preparation, so she probably got it ready back when she was still alive. After all, you never know when you're going to bite it in our line of work."

"Do you have any idea what it might have been?"

"No, not a clue. I went through all her personal effects in Heat Haze Palace after she died, but none of what I found comes to mind..."

Klaus went silent as he dug through his memory, but he still couldn't come up with anything.

Thea gave him a pained smile. "Maybe she hid it somewhere that not even you knew about."

"It's certainly possible. I mean, this is the boss we're talking about. She would have had no compunctions about hiding something important under the floor or something."

"In that case, shall we tear down the walls once we get back?"

"Let's not go that far. Still, it wouldn't hurt to look through her room one more—"

Klaus stopped mid-sentence.

The moment he did, Thea's eyes went wide.

The two of them had just remembered the incident that had happened one month prior.

They groaned in unison. ""Oh no, that's the room that—""

When the ferry arrived in the Din Republic, Klaus and Thea went back to Heat Haze Palace well ahead of the others. Their destination was the bedroom in the middle of the second floor, the one that was slightly larger than all the others.

A month had passed, but it was still just as demolished as it had been the last time they saw it.

Thanks to Annette's bomb, Lily's bedroom had been blown to smithereens. All they'd done so far was hang a tarp over the wall. They hadn't gotten around to actually repairing anything yet, and the room was still covered in cracks and burn marks.

Klaus headed over to the tattered wall, felt around for spots where the damage was especially severe, and smashed through them with his knife. Thea followed his lead and started looking through the rifts in the broken floor.

The first one to unearth something was Klaus. "Found it."

He retrieved a small iron box from inside the wall. There was no way they would have found it if Annette hadn't blown up the room. Apparently, every cloud had its silver lining.

"Go ahead and open it, Thea. I'm almost certain this was her gift to you."

"Will do…"

Klaus handed her the box, and Thea took a deep breath.

This was the final thing Hearth had left behind.

Her fingers trembled with anticipation as she gingerly opened the lid.

Inside, there was a peculiar little rod of some sort. It was long, brass, and bumpy. Thea had never seen it before, but she knew what it reminded her of.

"Is this…a key?"

It was her first time seeing a key that looked like that, but it was definitely a key of some sort.

She showed it to Klaus, but he just tilted his head as well. He didn't know what it was for, either.

The box also had a small card down at the very bottom.

To the girl who will surpass me.

Short as the message was, it conveyed everything it needed to.

Thea could feel the corners of her eyes start to go hot.

Their reunion would never come. Hearth's kindness had died with her, and Thea's dream of getting to live alongside her would never come to fruition. Their relationship had ended in the saddest way imaginable.

Yet, even despite that, Hearth had left her so much.

"Teach…" Thea's voice was trembling. "Just this once, could you lend me your chest?"

Klaus said nothing. He just gently reached over and stroked Thea's head, then held her close as she sobbed her eyes out.

Around the time Thea finished crying, the rest of the team began returning as well.

They all ended up trickling into the destroyed room where Klaus and Thea were. They looked at Thea quizzically upon seeing how red and puffy her eyes were, but they quickly read the room and patted her on the back.

Once they were all assembled, Lily clapped her hands together. "All righty! We just finished a big mission, so now's a perfect time to put my room back together!"

Fixing up Lily's room had sort of been put on the back burner.

The thing was, the girls didn't have the skill sets to perform repairs that extensive, so they were going to need to call in a professional. Fortunately, there were contractors who specialized in working with spies and other clients where confidentiality was imperative.

As Lily started muttering greedily about wanting to perform some renovations, too, Thea decided to make her request. "Lily, I actually had a favor I was hoping to ask. Would you be willing to trade rooms with me?"

"Huh? What do you mean?"

"It would mean a lot to me to be able to live in Ms. Hearth's old room. What do you say? If you moved into my room, you wouldn't have to wait for the repairs."

Thea tilted her head and gave Lily a coaxing smile.

Lily responded by furrowing her brow. "Hrmm... I get how you feel, I really do. But at the same time, this one's pretty roomy, and it gets a bunch of natural sunlight..."

"What if I offered to teach you how to pick up guys?"

"What makes you think I would even want that?"

It looked like the quarrel over the room was about to get heated.

That was when Grete stepped in. "I think you both have it wrong," she said. "If anyone is going to have Hearth's old room, shouldn't it be the boss?"

Everyone turned to look at Klaus.

Klaus had been using the same room since his days with Inferno, and to be blunt, it wasn't a very nice one. It was a cramped room stuck in a far corner of the manor.

He shook his head. Then, for good measure, he added his usual, "And don't call me 'Boss.'"

Whenever Grete referred to him as "Boss," Klaus shot her down without fail. In his eyes, the only person worthy of that title was Hearth. He had rejected being called that since the day he founded Lamplight, and he had probably avoided inheriting Hearth's room for much the same reason.

This time, though, Grete held firm. "I think you're wrong there, Boss. I think that by this point, you're this team's boss in every sense of the word."

"Hrmm..."

Klaus didn't have an immediate reply to that.

As he mulled over how best to respond, Annette piped up with her thoughts. "I agree with her, Bro." She laughed.

Erna shared the sentiment. "Me too."

Sybilla gave Klaus's arm an amused shove. "C'mon, man. All of us are graduatin', so maybe it's time for you to graduate from that wishy-washy position of yours, too."

Graduation.

Before the mission, Klaus had told the girls that once they completed it, they would become full-fledged spies.

Now they had done just that, and they'd demonstrated how much they'd all grown to boot. The team still had a number of shortcomings, but they were all strong enough to pass a spy academy graduation exam. The girls had improved far faster than Klaus could have imagined.

They were all ready to advance to the next stage of their careers.

The battle against Serpent was only going to get harder, and for that matter, Serpent might not be the only enemy they were going to have to confront. They would probably come face-to-face with all sorts of other fierce foes, as well.

The girls were right. It was time for Klaus to steel his resolve, too.

His boss was gone, and she wasn't coming back. Now, leading the girls was up to him.

"No, you're right. I *am* Lamplight's boss," Klaus said with great dignity.

He was a spy, he was a teacher, and, yes, he was their boss.

Lily laughed. "I mean, I'm too used to calling you 'Teach' to change now."

"Hey, I'm just glad you finally get it, Klaus," Monika said pompously.

"I'll be countin' on you, Boss," Sybilla said, sounding a little bashful.

"At long last, my wish finally came true...Boss," Grete said with a nod.

Sara bowed. "I—I look forward to continuing to work with you, B-Boss."

"You'll always be 'Bro' to me," Annette quipped, to which Erna agreed, "Yeah. You're Teach, Teach."

The final one to speak up was Thea. "I'm expecting great things out of you as my partner, Teach," she said with a smile.

"So I see there's no consensus to be reached."

The only ones who'd actually changed how they addressed him were Sybilla and Sara. That said, he was fine with them calling him whatever they wanted.

The point was, he knew where he stood.

"Magnificent," he murmured. It was a nice feeling.

Soon, the battle was going to advance to its next stage as well.

Afterword

I know that Volume 4 isn't the greatest place for it, but I hope you don't mind if I take a moment to talk about my writing process for Volume 3.

The thing about *Spy Classroom* is that when I began the series, I had this structure for the first four books laid out in my head. I was going to have all eight girls play a role in Volume 1, spend Volumes 2 and 3 doing deep dives on four of them apiece, and then have them come back together for a big mission in Volume 4. I had it planned out.

However, I spent all my time down to the last minute trying to figure out which girl to center Volume 4 around. I'm telling you, I was really racking my brain.

My original plan was to have it be Thea, but there was this other idea that I just couldn't get out of my head. *It really should be* her, *shouldn't it?* I kept thinking to myself.

That's right—I'm talking about Erna.

After all, wouldn't it be poetic? She shows up in the very first book, but due to her unique circumstances, she barely shows up in any of the illustrations, and as of right now, December 2020, she's been completely left out of all the merchandise offerings! She deserved to stand big and proud on the cover of season one's big finale! (And more to the point, I felt sorry for her.)

But then, as I was working on Volume 3, I realized something.

"Yeep!" "Yeep! "Yeep?" "Yeep!" "How unlucky..." "YEEP?!"

I could see the writing on the wall.

Yeah, this isn't the right spot for her...

I love her to bits, but Volume 4 wasn't really the kind of story that would let her shine, so she's going to have to wait a bit before she gets to be the lead. In the end, I went with Thea after all.

Now I have some news for you—at around the same time Volume 4 of *Spy Classroom* comes out, the first volume of SeuKaname's manga adaptation will be going on sale as well! Being a manga lets the scenes of the girls chatting with one another really pop, and it's crammed with all sorts of fantastic stuff I wasn't able to describe to its fullest in the light novel! (Annette and Erna are especially adorable in it.)

I actually wrote the manga script from scratch, and starting from the back half of the manga's first volume, there's going to be a whole bunch of completely manga-original content. There were a bunch of scenes I wanted to do that relied on the manga format to work, and thanks to all of SeuKaname's help, we were able to pull them off. Granted, Seu-Kaname did most of the work, but still. Chapter 5 was a particular favorite of mine.

Here at the end, I have one last announcement I'd like to make. Starting with the next book, *Spy Classroom* will be entering its second season. Pretty exciting, right? Originally, I included a little "Next Mission" teaser at the end of Volume 4, but that part got nixed for being too much of a cliffhanger and for "ruining all the catharsis!" My editor came at me pretty hard for that one.

Anyhow, the girls' next battle is going to be a harsh one, so I hope you look forward to it. The key word to look out for is *weakling*. Until then, though, that's all from me.

Takemachi

HAVE YOU BEEN TURNED ON TO LIGHT NOVELS YET?

86—EIGHTY-SIX, VOL. 1–10

In truth, there is no such thing as a bloodless war. Beyond the fortified walls protecting the eighty-five Republic Sectors lies the "nonexistent" Eighty-Sixth Sector. The young men and women of this forsaken land are branded the Eighty-Six and, stripped of their humanity, pilot "unmanned" weapons into battle...

Manga adaptation available now!

WOLF & PARCHMENT, VOL. 1–6

The young man Col dreams of one day joining the holy clergy and departs on a journey from the bathhouse, Spice and Wolf. Winfiel Kingdom's prince has invited him to help correct the sins of the Church. But as his travels begin, Col discovers in his luggage a young girl with a wolf's ears and tail named Myuri who stowed away for the ride!

Manga adaptation available now!

SOLO LEVELING, VOL. 1–5

E-rank hunter Jinwoo Sung has no money, no talent, and no prospects to speak of—and apparently, no luck, either! When he enters a hidden double dungeon one fateful day, he's abandoned by his party and left to die at the hands of some of the most horrific monsters he's ever encountered.

Comic adaptation available now!